FORGET ME NOT

W WINTERS

AUTHOR'S COPYRIGHT

SYNOPSIS

I fell in love with a boy a long time ago. I was only a small girl. Scared and frightened, I was taken from my home and held against my will. His father hurt me, but *he* protected me and kept me safe as best he could.

Until I left him.

I ran the first chance I got and even though I knew he wasn't behind me, I didn't stop. The branches lashed out at me, punishing me for leaving him in the hands of a monster.

I've never felt such guilt in my life.

Although I survived, the boy was never found. I prayed for him to be safe. I dreamed he'd be alright and come back to me. Even as a young girl I knew I loved him, *but I betrayed him.*

Twenty years later, all my wishes came true.

But the boy came back a man. With a grip strong enough to keep me close and a look in his eyes that warned me to never dare leave him again. I was his to keep, after all.

Twenty years after leaving one hell, I entered another. Our tale was only just getting started.

It's dark and twisted.

But that doesn't make it any less of what it is.

A love story. *Our* love story.

SOMETHING TO REMEMBER

PREQUEL TO FORGET ME NOT

CHAPTER 1

I used to wonder what I'd done to deserve this. Why he hates me so much.

My stomach rumbles, and the aching pain that used to make me ball up because it was centered in my stomach now shoots through my body. I wince from the pain, but I don't scream. The stinging in my eyes isn't from tears. I refuse to shed them.

I've made my choice.

This room, in particular, is one I used to be terrified of. Cinder block walls that are damp and cold, and nothing but a blanket to cover me when I sleep on the hard cement floor. The fluorescent lights are horribly bright, and they remind me of the school's gym lights, but somehow the darkness, when he shuts them off makes the lights unbearable when they're on.

There's nowhere to hide when the lights are on.

I lick my dry lips as the pain settles and stare at the steel door until I feel like I can breathe easy again. I'm no longer afraid of the room. The punishment holding, as my father calls it. It will be my salvation. My escape from what fate has offered me.

Even at fourteen years old, I know what life and death are all too well.

I know my mother's dead. She never hears me when I scream for her. And I always do. I always cry out for her to save me when he makes me hurt and doesn't stop.

A chill runs through my body, but at the same time my forehead heats and a thin sweat covers my skin. I shudder and think about pulling the blanket up, but the blinking red light in the corner of the room reminds me that he's watching and I won't show him that I'm trying anymore.

I don't want comfort. I don't want to hope anymore. They're both useless and make trying and fighting seem reasonable when they aren't.

Maybe death is an exaggeration. After all I'm starving myself, and he's thrown me in here with the promise of food if I'll eat. I don't want to though. I can't keep living like this.

This isn't a life. When my mother died, it was my death sentence to be left in the hands of a monster.

Another spike of pain shoots through me at the same time as I hear the keys jingle on the other side of the steel door. I resist the urge to react to the pain although it's stronger and more intense than it's ever been.

I wish it weren't true, but even as I've accepted death as my fate, I'm terrified. I wish it wasn't fear that ran through me. I wish the adrenaline wouldn't spike in my blood and my natural instinct wasn't to cower, but I can't help it.

I've tried hard not to feel anymore, but the fear he's instilled in me is unbreakable.

Maybe that's why I hate myself so much. I'm weak and useless. Just like he tells me.

Some days I swear I don't feel anything anymore. Even the fear. It's as if it doesn't matter, like I don't matter anymore. How can I? How could I even be sane staring at the same walls each and every day? I barely move anymore. It must be days since I've decided not to eat. And since that day I've been in this room. Unmoving, unchanging other than the pain.

It's only a matter of time before he'll let me out of this room. It's just for punishments, or at least that's what it used to be. I don't know how many consecutive days I've been in here. Maybe it's my new home.

I scratch my fingernail against the cement, creating a mark. There are dozens of lines just like it. I think I started them to count the days, but it's turned into something else. Each one is the same as the last. Maybe I'm waiting for something to change them. Something inside of me or inside of this room to break up the monotony. Maybe I've just stopped caring.

I think Father's easier on me when I'm pathetic like this. It makes me feel even worse knowing he's the reason, he's the motivating factor behind it all.

I blink slowly and my thick lashes blur the faint light from the small window as the door opens with a protesting groan.

I expect the door to close just as fast as it opens, but when I chance a glance, he's left it open. His large body stands in the doorway, and his dingy off-white shirt and faded jeans are dirty from working outside on the farm and in the dirt.

His boots sound as if they're crunching against the ground as he walks. Each step getting louder and my heart racing faster. I stay perfectly still, resisting every instinct to run or to fight. Both are useless.

"Get up," he says and his voice is deep and rough. No room for negotiation.

My body flinches out of instinct, and I prepare for him to kick me when I don't react quickly enough. He always kicks me in the stomach and as I close my eyes tightly, disobeying him, I pray he does it hard enough to end this.

But nothing comes.

With the thin coat of sweat over every inch of my body, a chill goes through me, making my body stiffen. I nearly vomit from the intensity of the change, but I hold back.

"I've had enough of this, boy!" my father screams at me and I curl into myself. Embarrassment and shame flow through me from how weak I am, but I don't give it much thought. I already knew I was pitiful.

"I won't fucking tell you again!" he yells and leans down to haul me up by my shirt, but I scoot back and resist. If there's one thing I've learned never to do, it's to resist.

But I've wanted this. I have to remind myself of my death wish as the fear cripples me and the years of conditioning settle in and make my body tremble.

The back of his large, dirty hand whirls in front of my face, blurring from the speed as he snarls at me. The scowl on his face is only made more terrifying from his exposed yellowed teeth and the coldness in his dark gaze.

The last thing I see are his knuckles.

The last thing I hear is the crunch of my nose.

The last thing I taste is the metallic blood in my mouth.

THE LAST THING I FEEL IS NOTHING. SO LONG I'VE WAITED for it. And it's finally here.

CHAPTER 2

*F*uck.

My neck is stiff, my jaw hurts and I know it's bruised. But what really fucking hurts is my throat. It's worse than a sore throat, raw and like it's on fire.

A groan slips out and I instantly regret it, my body squirming on a hard sheet of metal. I blink slowly, barely opening them and letting my eyes adjust to the dim light.

I know in an instant where I am. The kitchen.

The dusty plaid curtain on the window above the sink is the first thing I see, and that's all I need to know.

The kitchen, the table. Mother.

This is where she was a few times, I remember it well but I don't know what brought her here. Maybe it was him. I never thought about it back then, but as my eyes open wider, anger seeps in. *Did he hurt her like he hurt me?*

My muscles coil, and I try to sit up.

It only lasts a moment and then the pain in my throat makes me wince again.

Shit. It's only when I lift my hand to my throat that I

realize the pain is only located there. It's no longer focused on my stomach in the least.

"I had to intubate you," my father says from the dark corner of the room. My heart thuds hard in my chest as he slowly stands and walks into the light of the room.

"Stupid fucking boy," he mutters and stands next to me. So close I can smell the dirt and whiskey that waft from him every day.

I try to swallow, but it only makes my dry throat hurt even worse. A sickness and hollowness threaten me. I can't even kill myself. I'm that pathetic.

I need to find another way then. Something fast.

"You need to knock this shit off," my father says as though he heard my thoughts. My heart stutters as I slowly raise my eyes to his. I don't dare speak though.

He looks tired up here with the morning light casting shadows down his face. He rubs his beard and clucks his tongue once before lowering his head to mine.

I instinctively back away as he says in a low voice, a roughness from his throat making his threat sound even more terrifying, "Don't make this harder on yourself than it has to be, you hear?"

Like the coward I am, I nod. My blood rushing and fueled by fear.

"I have something for you," he says as he backs away slowly. One step and then another, giving me space, but I don't trust it. "Sit up," he tells me. My body's stiff and my muscles sore. It hurts, it physically hurts to stay still, but I'm done with this.

Just let me die.

"Sit up!" my father screams, pounding his fists so close

to my legs and rattling the table. My body jolts as I stare at his face, bright red as he spits, "Sit the fuck up!"

He grips my shoulders with a bruising force and rips me up so quickly my ass lifts off the table and for a moment I think he'll throw me off. Maybe into the old walnut cupboards. But he doesn't. *Thump, thump, thump,* my heart races, but I push down the fear.

There's nothing he can do to me anymore.

There's nothing left to take.

My shoulders shake uncontrollably, making me feel even weaker as he looks me in the eyes and reaches into his back pocket. It's a wrinkled polaroid picture, and I can't help how my eyes dart to it and then to his face. I wait, still as stone and cold as one too as he flicks it with his fingers, not showing me fully and teasing me with it.

I don't know what it could be. Really anything, I suppose. Whatever it is, it's a threat and it won't work. There's nothing more threatening than simply living at this point.

He flicks it again and the thwack of the paper just annoys me. My teeth grind together as I slowly turn away from him. It doesn't matter. Whatever he has to threaten me with, I don't care. It'll all be over soon.

My throat seems to clench, painfully scraping as I take in a sharp breath. The sight of my father's hand so close to my face prepares me for the inevitable blow. But it doesn't come. It's only when he takes a step away that I finally look down at my lap. The photo is face down against my worn dirtied jeans and I almost don't pick it up.

Almost. But the curiosity is too strong.

I flip it over, prepared for the worst, but my forehead scrunches when I realize what it is.

It's just a girl. Huddled into a small ball, her t-shirt and jeans are dirty like she's been dragged through the mud. Her sneakers are still on her as well. It takes a moment for me to understand what I'm seeing, but when I do, my heart stops beating right. She's in my room. That cement floor is the same floor I was just sleeping on.

She's in the punishment room.

"Get her out," I say and the words are pushed through my lips the second they reach me as a thought. I will my tired body to move, but my father's quicker than I am. So fast that the back-hand smacks against my cheek and mouth, splitting my lip open and flinging my head backward. My body flails as I attempt to stay on the raised metal table, but my fingers slip along the smooth metal and I fall. I stumble down on the ground, my side hitting the knob of a cupboard on the way down and my elbow landing hard on the linoleum floor.

I suck in a breath between clenched teeth, but remain still on the floor. Not daring to move from my awkward position. Another lesson my father has taught me well.

My heart races in my chest, feeling as though it's trying to get away. Trying to go to her. But I stay still.

I need to listen. "Don't hurt her," I say the words in a hoarse voice but it's nothing but a plea. A pathetic plea that will fall on deaf ears. "Please," I add weakly and hang my head.

I don't want her hurt. No one should ever go into that room. It's a place for nightmares and monsters. Maybe my father should be locked away in that cell. But not her.

I chance a peek up at my father, watching as he nods slightly and then runs his fingers over his jawline. His knuckles are split from striking me and the knowledge makes me smile slightly. But I hide it. The tip of my tongue runs along the cut on my lip as I look down and away, trying to remember every detail of the girl on the floor.

"Is she okay?" I dare to ask him.

"Fine," he says gruffly, stopping in his tracks and walking toward me. He has to shove the table to the side in the narrow kitchen to bend down close to me. Again his scent drifts toward me, and this time it's stronger. So strong I nearly vomit, but I hold it back.

"She's going to be good. I already know that," he says and I can feel his eyes on me. Waiting for a reaction and my response.

Whatever I do, I need to save her from this fate. I take a steadying breath, making sure I don't react in the least. I just need to get to her.

"Do you want to see her?" my father asks. "I got her for you."

Finally, my eyes reach his and my chest rises with a disbelieving breath.

"All you have to do is listen. And she's yours." I watch as the smile slowly stretches across his face as he adds, "Listen to me and she stays safe."

CHAPTER 3

I want to get closer to her, but I stay right where I am.

I can see she's breathing, and that's what matters right now.

Listen to me and she stays safe. My father's words echo in my head repeatedly as I wait for her to awaken. I was desperate to get in here. I needed to see her to protect her, but with every second that passes... I start to hate her.

I was so ready to give in. So ready to end all this shit. And now, because of her, my fate is worse than it's ever been.

Yet, so much better.

My fingers itch to push her hair away from her face. She's young; younger than me, I'm sure. She's pretty in a traditional sense. Her hair is ruffled though, and she needs to be taken care of.

There's a scratch on her cheek, like a scrape more than a scratch I guess.

My back leans against the cinder block wall, and it's

cold and hard, but it's giving me stability. The thing I hate most about this situation, is that I'm still helpless.

There used to be ointment in the medicine cabinet. The mirror has a patina from where you have to grip the edge to open it. But in the old mirror cabinet, there was an ointment for scratches. I don't know if there is now.

A weak humorless smile makes the corner of my lip twitch as I pick at the frayed end of my jeans. I can't even get her something for the scrape.

Pathetic.

That hasn't changed in the least.

She doesn't know though. She doesn't know anything beyond these walls. I lean my head back, tearing my eyes away from her for the first time since I've been let back in.

She doesn't know. And she needs someone to protect her, even if it is only just enough to prevent a worse fate. Surely, it'll be enough?

For her. My teeth grind together and my knuckles turn white as I ball them into fists.

It better be enough. It has to be. It's all I have to offer, and now she's changed everything.

CHAPTER 4

Robin

My head hurts so badly. Why does it hurt so much? I try to push myself upright, and the ground is so cold and hard. It's so uncomfortable, but my head is too heavy and I slump against the ground.

Where am I?

I try to remember where I was. The sound of the carousel shrieking as it slowly turned from the wind blowing filters through my memory. The empty swings sway back and forth. The school playground is deserted. I thought everyone would be here today. But it's empty. The first day of summer and not a soul is here.

I remember how I looked up and the sun was far off in the distance, but still in the sky. Didn't they know we still had time to play? I'm younger than most of the kids, only twelve, but even the older ones usually play with me.

I sat on the swings for a while, I remember that. As the

pounding in my head throbs harder I remember how the metal chains twisted and I let myself twirl on the swings over and over. I could wait for the other kids. I was sure they'd show up.

Did they?

I squint, trying to remember and I turn my head. My palms brush against the concrete floor, my cheek flat against the hard floor.

There was a man. He had a golf club and he needed my help. I remember how lost he looked. He said he hit his last ball into the trees and he couldn't reach into the bushes.

My heartbeat quickens as I remember, and my body goes still.

I knew to tell him a lie. I knew to turn around and run when he tried to take my hand in his. But he looked so hurt when I tried to pull away. He was genuinely upset, and all he did was ask me to help him.

The thin branches cracked under my sneakers as I went into the woods, following him to where he thought the ball had landed.

I open my eyes and I can't breathe.

He lied to me. My nails scratch on the ground as I clench them into fists and slowly look up.

No! Mommy, help me! Tears blur my vision of the cinder block walls.

No! This can't be happening. I pull my knees into my chest and try to stand.

Why does my head hurt so much?

"Are you okay?" a soft voice asks from behind me, making me shuffle across the ground and push myself against the cold wall. It takes a moment for me to wipe my eyes and see him.

He's just a boy.

His knees are knobby and he's thin, but his shoulders are broad and he has a look about him that lets me know he's older than me. There's another look about him, too.

Sorrow and sadness cloud his eyes. Or maybe I just imagined it, because the moment my vision focuses, a hard expression stares back at me. He doesn't move from where he is, crouching only a few feet from me.

"Where am I?" I ask him quickly. I don't know where the words come from. I feel hot and cold, and I'm so confused. "I want to leave."

He huffs and shakes his head at me, pushing himself up from the ground where he was and takes a step toward me. He's taller than me. In that moment, he scares me.

"You can't leave," he says simply.

My face crumples, and I shake my head. "My mother will-"

"We're stuck here!" he yells at me, the anger in his voice making me flinch. He stares at the wall behind me, his eyes flickering to the floor then back to me. "We can't leave."

As I start to protest, I hear a loud rough bark outside. It's followed by a series of vicious barks that continue unceasingly. It makes me whirl around and face the only window. It's small and rectangular, covered in filth and high up on the wall. There's barely any light coming through. Maybe there's a bush planted in front of it. I'm not sure, but at the very least I know there are dogs close.

"Don't try to run," the boy says behind me and again I

turn to face him. Threats all around me, and it's my fault. It's all my fault. So stupid! I wrap my arms around my shoulders. "My mother-"

"Stop." The boy gives me the command, and I do. I stop because I'm a good girl. I've always been a good girl, but look at where it's gotten me.

It's quiet for a while, and the boy takes another step closer to me. I don't move. I don't know what to do or where I am, but deep down inside of me I know this boy isn't going to hurt me. There's something about him. Something broken and scared and angry even, but it's pure.

"What's going to happen to us?" I ask him weakly.

"He won't touch you. It's not about you."

"What?" I don't understand. I'm so confused.

"He's using you." He looks past me, anger evident as he clenches his jaw. "It's about him making me do what he wants. He knows I won't...," his voice drifts off, and the anger changes to something else. Something I can't see because he turns away from me.

I reach out to him, grabbing his arm to keep him from leaving me, moving purely out of instinct. The touch feels like a spark. As if I've put my hand to a flame, but before I can even process it, he whips back to me, a scowl of anger on his face as he stares at me. "I won't let him hurt you like he does me. All you are is a tool for him to use against me."

He takes another step closer to me, and it's the first time I really get a good look in his eyes. The intensity almost makes me scoot back, but then I'd be against the wall. Trapped and cornered.

He parts his lips to tell me something, but no words come out. Time passes, and the only thing I can hear is my heartbeat as he stares at me. His eyes won't break from mine, and I'm too scared to look away.

"I'm sorry," he says flatly, but then he turns away as if the sentiment were genuine.

For some reason, just hearing those words is what breaks me. The tears fall and as I wipe them away, he looks at me with distaste. I half expect him to tell me to stop, but he doesn't.

I struggle to calm myself and somehow I do. Maybe it's because I don't really believe him. I don't believe it's hopeless. My mother will find me, and she'll make that man pay for what he's done. Both to me and to this boy. I know she will.

"What's your name?" I ask to keep him from leaving me as he turns. I lick my lips, tasting the salty tears and wiping my cheeks. I don't want to cry. I want to get out of here.

"J-" he starts to answer me, but we both whip around and face the door as it opens, silencing us and making me instinctively back away.

I grab onto the boy's arm and force myself behind him. I don't know a thing about him and the look he gives me nearly makes me run from both him and the man stalking into the room, but I don't get the chance. The boy grips my wrist with his other hand and pulls me closer to him, my front to his back and my back to the wall. He keeps himself deliberately positioned in between me and the man.

It's only when I grab onto the boy, my small fingers

digging into the rough denim of his jeans at his hip and my cheek pressed against his back, that he lets go of me.

THE BOY MAY SCARE ME SOME, BUT THE MAN TERRIFIES ME.

CHAPTER 5

THAT NIGHT

"I want to go home," the girl whimpers. Her wide doe eyes dart from mine every time I look at her. We're on opposite sides of the room, and that's how it's been since I came back. That's all she keeps saying as she's bundled up in the corner and crying.

She's terrified, and has every right to be. But after what my father's done to me, I don't want to look at her. Partly out of shame. Partly out of hate. I was only gone for an hour, but an hour is enough.

He did it on purpose. Taking me the moment she woke up, and showing her how easily he can break me. He knew what he was doing, and it worked. And I did nothing to stop him. No fight in me... for her. And now, I can't even look at her.

I can feel the bags under my eyes, the desperate need for sleep. But I can't. Not with her here and not knowing what my father will do next. I force my dry throat to swallow, the pain still present and lean my head against the cold wall as I stare at the door. Sleep's come easily to

21

me this past week when I had nothing left to give, but I won't let it take me now.

"Please, can you just tell him to let me go?" she asks weakly. I can see her lean forward slightly, hesitant and praying for mercy from me. But I can't do anything for her. I'm so fucking helpless, and it only makes me angrier. Doesn't she know I'm pathetic? My father made sure to show her as much.

"I just want to-"

"Stop it," I tell her harshly and hate myself even more. I glare at her, ready to tell her how she needs to be quiet. How there's no way out and that her crying is only going to piss me off, but then I see how glossy her eyes are, how her lips are turned down in a way that makes her seem even more vulnerable.

My heart beats in a weird way, like it's skipping instead of beating. It hurts and my stomach churns with a sickness at who I am. Who I've become. I don't want to be like this. I don't want to be this person.

"Jay," she says and I look up at her. Her voice is soft. It doesn't matter how angry she is with me or I with her, we're all each other has.

I stare at her, waiting for her to say something, but the tears fall down her cheeks. They don't even require her to blink.

"I'm scared," she whispers. Her voice is hoarse and her shoulders crumple inward. My blood rings with adrenaline to move, to go to her and cradle her in her arms. But I don't want her to touch me back.

"I said I'd look out for you, right?" I ask her. Offering her a small smile. It's not genuine in the least, but I try. I mean it. I will look out for her. I don't know what I've done, but I know she didn't do a damn thing wrong. "I won't let him hurt you," I tell her.

"How could he not?" she asks in a murmur and her voice cracks at the end. "He's a bad man," she says and then licks the tears from her lips. "Bad men do bad things." She wraps her arms around herself and then looks back at me with an expression I can't place.

My skin heats, every inch of it feeling like it's on fire. "I'm here," I tell her simply.

"Hold me please," she pleads with me, wiping the tears from her eyes and looking away. "I'm just scared and I need…" she shakes her head, not finishing her thought.

"You need to sleep," I say, finishing it for her and she whips her eyes to mine. There's nothing but fear in hers. Her body is stiff and she slowly looks at the door.

"I'm here," I tell her softly and offer a hand out to her. I don't know why I do, I shouldn't. But she's quick to crawl across the cement floor to me. She drags the blanket with her and glances at the door as she comes over to sit next to me. I keep my distance when her knee bumps into mine. I scoot away, keeping a gap between the two of us.

The look on her face is like I smacked her, and she immediately withdraws. "I don't like to be touched," I tell her with a tense jaw.

Her head lowers and she slowly pulls and tucks the blanket around her. She hesitantly offers a bit of it to me, which makes my lips tug up into a smirk and I shake my head.

I don't want to be anything close to warm. The chill

23

keeps me up at night. I nestle my back against the wall and stare straight ahead. She's close, and hopefully feeling better, but there's not much else I can do for now. I've already started calculating a way to sneak her out. If we both run, he can't get us both. *I just need a chance.* How many times have I prayed for just that, only to go unheard?

But Robin isn't tainted like me. Maybe fate will have mercy on her.

"Sorry," she barely whispers the word and my eyes are drawn to her as she huddles under the blanket. She doesn't look at me as I ask, "For what?"

"I didn't mean to touch you, it's just so cold," she answers weakly.

I stare at her a moment, only because it doesn't feel cold to me really. A little chilly, but then again, maybe she's not used to this. I snort a humorless laugh, a huff really at the thought and that gets her attention.

When she looks up, her eyes dart to the rip in my shirt.

My father did that on purpose, too. She slowly reaches her hand up and I grab her wrist, my fingers wrapping easily around her as a small gasp comes from her lips. "Don't," I warn her, my heart beating wildly.

Her eyes look back down, past the tattered cotton and at the smattering of scars.

"What happened?" she asks me with sadness so evident in her voice.

I want to shove her off my lap, to leave her in this filthy cell. But I don't. Instead I stay perfectly still until I can lower her arm back down. If I leave her, I have nothing.

She'll judge me. Pity me. And use me.

But I need her. Without her, I have nothing.

My eyes drift to the cement floor. I should tell her that I don't know how to really help her. But I can't.

"I want to leave, Jay," she says and her eyes beg me as well and I want to tell her I'll find a way. But I'll never lie to her.

"I do too," I tell her the truth. I can give her a small bit of it.

If I can find a way, I'll make sure she gets out of here.

I swear to it. I'll do whatever it takes.

It's the only thing I have to live for anymore.

PROLOGUE

Robin

I can wait here longer than he can stand to stay away. I know that much.

A small grin pulls at my lips as I pick at the thread on the comforter. Always picking and waiting. There's nothing else to do in this room.

My head lifts at the thought, drawing my eyes to the blinking red light. And he's always watching. The sight of the camera makes my stomach churn, but only for a moment.

The sound of heavy boot steps walking down the stairs outside the closed door makes my heart race. I stare at the doorknob, willing it to turn and bring him to me.

I've waited too long for him.

The sound of the door opening is foreboding. If anyone other than me was waiting for him, I'd assume they'd have terror in their hearts. But I know him. I understand it all. The pain, the guilt. I know firsthand what it's like when the monster is gone and you only have your own thoughts to fight. Your memories and regrets. It's all-consuming.

And there's no one who can understand you. No one you trust, whose words you can believe are genuine and not just disguised pity.

But he knows me, and I know him. Far too well; our pain is shared.

His broad shoulders fill the doorway and his dark eyes meet mine instantly. He barely touches the door and it closes behind him with a loud click that's only a hair softer than my wildly beating heart.

It's hard to swallow, but I do. And I ignore the heat, the quickened breath. I push it all down as he walks toward me, closing the space with one heavy step at a time.

He stops in front of me, but doesn't hesitate to cup my chin in his large hand and I lean into his comforting touch. I know to keep my own hands down though and I grip the comforter instead of him.

It's a violent pain that rips through me, knowing how scarred he is. So much so, that I have to hold back everything. I'm afraid of my words, my touch. He's so close to being broken beyond repair and I only want to save him, but I don't know how.

We're both damaged, but the tortured soul in front of me makes me feel everything. He makes me want to live and heal his tormented soul. But how can I, when I'm the one who broke him by running away?

"My little bird," he whispers and it reminds me of when we were children. When we were trapped together.

He's not the boy who protected me.

He's not the boy whose eyes were filled with a darkness barely tempered with guilt.

He's not the boy I betrayed the moment I had a chance.

He's a man who's taking what he wants.

AND THAT'S ME.

CHAPTER 1

Robin

One week before

"*D*octor Everly?" a soft voice calls out, breaking me from my distant thoughts as another early spring chill whips through my thin jacket and sends goosebumps down my body. I slowly turn my head to Karen. Her cheeks are a little too pink from a combination of the harsh wind and a heavy-handed application of blush, and the tip of her nose is a bright red.

I grip my thin jacket closer, huddling in it as if it can protect me from the brutal weather. It's too damn cold for spring, but I suppose I'd rather be cold and uncomfortable out here. Today especially.

I give Karen a tight smile, although I don't know why. It's not polite to smile out here, or is it? "How are you doing?" I ask her as she walks closer to me.

She nods her head, taking in a breath and looking past

me at the pile of freshly upturned dirt. "It hurts still. It's just so sad." Karen's only twenty-three, fresh out of college and new to this. I'm new to it too. Marie was the first patient I've had who killed herself.

Sad isn't the right word for it. Devastating doesn't even begin to describe what it feels like when a young girl in your care decides her life is no longer worth living.

I clear my throat and turn on the grass to face her. The thin heels of my shoes sink into the soft ground, and I have to balance myself carefully just to stand upright.

"It is," I tell Karen, not sure what else to say.

"How do you handle…" her voice drifts off.

I don't know how to answer her. My lips part and I shake my head, but no words come out.

"I'm so sorry, Robin," she says and Karen's voice is strong and genuine. She knows how much Marie meant to me. But it wasn't enough.

I try to give her an appreciative smile, but I can't. Instead, I clear my tight throat and nod once, looking back to where Marie's buried.

"Are you okay?" she asks me cautiously, resting a hand on my arm, trying to comfort me. And I do what I shouldn't. *I lie.*

"I'm okay," I tell her softly, reaching up to squeeze her hand.

As I tuck a loose strand of hair behind my ear, a gust of wind flies by us and a bolt of lightning splits the sky into pieces, followed a few seconds later with the hard crack of thunder.

Karen looks up, and in an instant the light gray clouds darken and cue the storm to set in. It's only the two of us left here and it looks like the weather won't have us here any longer, leaving Marie all alone. I think deep inside that's how she wanted it all along. She didn't want a shrink to give her advice.

Who was I to help her? The guilt washes through me and the back of my eyes prick with unshed tears as I take in a shuddering breath, shoving my hands in my pockets and turning back to her grave.

As much as I'd like to believe I'll let her rest now, I know I'll be back. It's selfish of me. She just wanted to be left alone. She needed that so her past could fade into the background. I know that now; I wish I knew it then.

"She's in a better place," Karen whispers and my gaze whips up to hers. She doesn't have the decency to look me in the eyes and I have to wonder if she just said the words because she thinks they're appropriate. Like it's something meant to be said when talking of the dead, or maybe she really believes it.

Karen turns to walk toward her car as the sprinkling of rain starts to fall onto us. She looks back over her shoulder, waiting for me and I relent, joining her.

I'm sorry, Marie.

As the cold drops of rain turn to sheets and my hair dampens, my pace picks up. It doesn't take long until we're both jogging through the grass and then onto the pavement of the parking lot, our heels clicking and clacking on the pavement with the sound of the rain.

I barely hear her say goodbye and manage a wave behind me as I open my car door and sink into the driver seat.

I just wanted to help Marie. I could see so much of

myself in her. We were almost the same age. She had the same look in her eyes. The same helplessness and lack of self-worth. I wanted to save her like my psychiatrist saved me.

But how could I? I'm not over my past. I should have known better. I should have referred her to someone more capable. Someone who had less emotional investment. I pushed too hard. *It's my fault.*

The pattering of rain on the car roof is eerily rhythmic as I dig through my purse, shivering and shoving the wet hair out of my face. The keys jingle as I shove them into the ignition, turning on the car and filling the cabin with the sounds of the radio.

I'm not sure what song's on but I don't care because I'm quick to turn the radio off. To get back to the silence and the peace of the rainfall. I slump in my seat, staring at the temperature gauge. When I look up, I see Karen drive away in the rearview mirror. Watching her car drive out of sight, my eyes travel to my reflection.

I scoff at myself and wipe under my eyes. I look dreadful. My dirty blonde hair's damp and disheveled, my makeup's running. I lift the console and grab a few tissues to clean myself up before sluggishly removing my soaked jacket and tossing it in the backseat. The heater finally kicks on, and I still can't bring myself to leave.

I look back into the mirror and see that I'm somewhat pulled together, but I can't hide the bags under my eyes. I can't force a false sense of contentment onto my face.

I close my eyes and take in another deep breath, filling my lungs and letting it out slowly. I need sleep. I need to eat. It's been almost a week since I found out about Marie.

A week of her no longer being here to call and check in on. Tears stream freely down my cheeks. I tried so hard not to cry; I learned a long time ago that crying doesn't help, but being forced to leave her is making me helpless to my emotions.

That first night I almost cried, but instead I resorted to sleeping pills. A wave of nausea churns in my stomach at the thought of what I did. It was so easy to just take one after the other. Each one telling me it'd be over soon. After downing half the bottle, I knew what I was doing. But the entire bottle was too much and it all came back up before I could finish it. Thank God for that. I'm not well, and I'm sure as hell not in a position to help others.

My hand rests against my forehead as I try to calm down, as I try to rid myself of the vision of Marie in my office, but other memories of my past persist there, waiting for this weakness.

I can't linger any longer. Putting the car into reverse, I back out of my spot, turning and seeing Marie's plot in the distance as I back up.

Grief is a process, but guilt is something entirely different. It's becoming harder and harder to separate the two, and I know why.

She reminds me of *him*.

Of a boy, I knew long ago. The turn signal seems louder than ever as I wait at the exit to turn onto the highway. *Click, click, click.*

Each is a second of time that I'm here and they're not. *Click, click, click.*

The cabin warms as I drive away, merging onto the highway.

Maybe all this has nothing to do with Marie.

Maybe it's just the guilt that summons the vision of his light gray eyes from the depths of my memory.

Maybe it's because I'm to blame for both of their deaths.

CHAPTER 2

John

The faint sounds of the radio disappear with a loud click as I shut it off. It's an old ass black box, covered in oil and grime from the shop, but it still works. Without it, the garage is silent. I wipe my hands with the blue shop towel, picking under my short, thick nails and scrub against the rough callus on my left thumb.

I'm a blue-collar mechanic, and there's not much more to me. Day in and day out, I work at my shop on the outskirts of town. The old oak trees and converted barn on the far side of the property are everything I need. I like my peace and quiet out here. I'd be a liar if I said I didn't get a bit lonely at times, but I don't need companionship. I don't need anyone.

I turn to look over my shoulder at the banged-up cherry red Chevy truck. That's going to take a bit of work tomorrow when Steve gets in. Fixing that side door would be a pain in my ass to do alone. And now that Steve's gone home, it's just me.

That damn truck can wait till tomorrow.

All the tools are back where they belong except for a few wrenches on the bench. The shop itself is old, with a cracked concrete floor and chipped red paint on the far wall where the hangar's attached to the garage. When I bought this place, it was rundown and in desperate need of fixing up. I love the charm of it though, how it's beaten down but still standing strong. The history is what I look forward to when I come here every day. The property itself is large. An old pilot used to live here. He loved two things in his life, the ducks on the lake out back and his airplanes in the hangar.

Poor old man didn't live long after he sold the place to me. I've still got an old Ercoupe from the 1940s he left here. I meant to fix it up, but time's gotten away from me and work's been steady.

I toss the cloth onto the bench and stretch my back, reaching my arms over my head and letting out a deep sigh. My back cracks, and it feels damn good. It's been a long day of hard work. And I'll have another one tomorrow. That's what I live for.

The dim evening light streams through the open garage door, bringing a crisp breeze with it. It feels relaxing. I take in a deep breath and close my eyes, feeling the exhaustion flow through me. I don't know the last time I had a good night's sleep. Doesn't matter how many hours I seem to get, I'm never well rested.

I pull the thin, dirty white t-shirt over my head, feeling my sore muscles stretch even more. My denim jeans sit low on my hips. They're dirtied too, but I don't give a damn about them. I ball up the shirt and rag, tossing them into the bin and get ready for the short walk up the hill and to my house on the other side of the dirt road.

The familiar sound of the door to the shop creaking snaps my eyes open. My body tenses, and my muscles coil. The shop's closed, and there's no one else out here for miles. There isn't a single reason anyone should be walking through my shop right now. I can hear heavy boot steps walking back here to the garage.

I straighten my broad shoulders as I slowly and silently pick up the largest wrench on the bench, my eyes staring straight ahead at the open door to the garage. The cold metal easily slips into my palm, feeling just right as my heart thumps and my breathing steadies. I only make it a single step when Jay steps into the doorway.

He's just as tall as me, which would be intimidating to most. My arms are corded with muscle from years of hard work and manual labor. As are his, although I haven't got the faintest idea what he does. I've never asked.

We're both daunting men, the difference is that I try to hide it. I'm not looking for a fight or to scare anyone. I'm not sure Jay is either, but he can't hide the darkness inside him or the terror of his past that eats away at him.

There's a softness about my eyes and a gentleness in my rough voice. It's enough to make people comfortable enough with me to get along just fine. There's not a damn bit of that in Jay. There's a hard edge in his eyes that never leaves. His shoulders turn in just slightly like he's ready to fight at all times. He could maybe fool you with charm, since he's got some of that in him, but the way his eyes pierce through you is enough to send a chill down your spine.

I'm usually not intimidated or frightened by anyone. I can stand on my own and take care of myself when I have to. But Jay has a side of him I'm pissed to admit frightens me. Not because of what he'd do to me, since I know I can take him. And not because I think he'd come for me. I toss the wrench down on the old wooden bench and start walking toward him, wiping my palms down on my jeans.

Jay's not a threat to me; he's not my enemy.

The fear is because I never know what Jay's going to do. He's fucked up in the head from his old man. Anger management doesn't even begin to describe what he needs. He's got problems I don't know how to handle, and it doesn't matter how much I try to help him. Some things you just can't fix.

Nonetheless, Jay's been there for me when I had no one. And I know why he's the way he is. I don't see him much, especially not since I picked up and moved to this tiny ass town, but if he needs me, I won't turn my back on him.

Jay's eyes light up and a smirk plays at his lips as he saunters down the wooden steps to the garage and gestures at the wrench. "You think that'd stop me?" he asks with playfulness in his voice.

I grin back at him, stopping to lean against the Chevy's cargo bed in the middle of the large garage and shrugging my shoulders. A rough chuckle vibrates up my chest and I look back to my hands.

Jay's boots smack on the floor as he comes to my side,

bracing a hand on the back end of the truck and looking over his shoulder at the door.

"You bring someone with you?" I ask him.

He frowns a bit, shaking his head and looking down at the ground. He never comes with anyone. I may be a loner to some extent, but Jay is something different. I'm not sure if he prefers it that way, or if it's because he just doesn't trust himself.

"I got a favor to ask." He stands beside me, shoving his hands into his jeans pockets and leaning back against the truck with me, mirroring my posture. He stares straight ahead and runs the back of his hand over his nose before saying, "You can't tell anyone." His voice is deadly low, and it makes my blood freeze in my veins.

I stare at him, waiting for more, but nothing comes. I clear my throat and try to relax against the hard metal.

I crack my neck to the side and nod my head. "You know I'm not going to say shit, Jay."

He nods his head slightly, his brow furrowing as he continues to avoid my gaze. He swallows thickly and says, "I'm gonna do something... and I need your help."

He finally looks at me, his eyes as cold as ice and narrowed. "There's a woman." My heart thuds once and my hands start to clench into fists, but I keep it from happening. Every bit of me is screaming to back out now, to tell him I don't want to hear it.

But I know what he's capable of, and I need to know who she is and what he's planning.

"A woman?" I ask. A chill flows in waves down my arms as if a cold draft has come through. I ignore the churning in the pit of my stomach. He'd never hurt a woman. Never. I know him. There's no fucking way he'd ever put his hand on a woman.

"She's broken, John." His voice is full of pain, and he breaks the gaze first. He talks to the ground as he adds, "She needs my help, but she's not going to want it."

"Then don't," I answer simply. If she doesn't want the help, there's no fucking reason he should approach her. He's got a warped sense of reality.

"She's hurting because of me," he admits quietly.

Tension grows in every inch of my body. I focus on my breathing, on staying cool and calm. Jay's violent and hot tempered. I stretch my jaw and look away, trying to convince myself it's going to be okay. That I can change his mind or stop him from whatever fucked up bullshit he thinks is going to happen.

"I have to," he says with conviction as if he read my mind.

It's only then that I see the dark circles under his eyes and how weary he looks. "Maybe you-" I speak without thinking, just trying to keep him appeased and take control of the situation.

"No," he interrupts, shaking his head before I can even finish. His body looks just as tense as mine as he pushes off the truck. I think he's going to leave, but instead, he starts pacing, running his hands through his thick short hair. "It's because of me," he confesses without stopping as his strangled voice repeats in nearly a whisper, "It's because of me."

My chest squeezes tight with pain watching him like this. It's been years. I haven't seen him break down since we were children. *Weak. Pathetic.*

The words whisper in the back of my head and he stops in his tracks, turning slowly, giving me a deadly look as if I said them out loud. For a moment, I think I may have. But he relaxes his stance and walks toward me slowly, stopping a few feet from me.

"She needs help."

"Then get her help from someone else." I answer him simply, licking my lower lip and hoping he'll reconsider whatever his plans are.

His eyes narrow slightly as he cocks his head, an asymmetric grin growing on his face. "She's going to help me, too." The way he says the words, so softly, with so much confidence and conviction, forces me to stare into his eyes, realizing there's no way to get him to stop.

"What are you going to do?" I ask, crossing my arms and trying my damnedest to just stay calm.

"I just want to get her alone and talk to her."

"Kidnapping-" The word is ripped from my throat before he cuts me off.

"It's not what you think," he says, his own hands balling into fists so tightly his knuckles turn white. The air is tense and thick between us. The sun setting makes the garage darker than it was only moments ago.

"You want me to help you kidnap her?" I ask him, not bothering to hide the disgust in my voice. The smile stays in place on his lips as he searches my eyes for something. He reaches into his pocket and pulls out a folded photograph. It's been creased twice, once down the middle and again at an angle off-center. He smooths it in his palm, finally looking away from me and answering, "I don't need help there, John." His voice is sad, as if he already regrets taking her.

He passes me the photo, flattening it against my chest with a hard thud and not letting go until I reach up to take the photo with my own hand.

"I just want you there to watch."

Adrenaline pumps through me at his request, anger rising in me. "And what am I going to be watching?"

"I just want to talk to her. I don't want to hurt her. I just want to fix her."

"Then get her help-"

"She's a shrink now," he says quickly. His eyes water slightly and he sniffs, looking away to take in a ragged breath. He licks his lower lip and looks back at me, willing me to understand. "She tried to kill herself," he says in an even voice I don't trust. "She grew up okay, you know?" He shakes his head once and pinches the bridge of his nose. "I didn't know she wasn't okay. I didn't know." I don't know if he's talking to me or to himself. His face is scrunched up with genuine pain.

"Who is she?"

"She's just a girl. I broke her, and I need to fix her." The strength in his tone solidifies his plan. He wraps his hand around the thin railing to the steps and mutters under his breath so low I almost don't hear him as he walks away, "And she's going to fix me."

"You won't do this without me?" I yell at his back, more a command than a question. I'll figure out something to keep him from doing this. I have to.

He turns to look over his shoulder, his face all raw pain and agony. He nods his head once. "I have to do this, but you need to be there. For me and her, John." His eyes dart to the floor, then back to me. "I'm going tomorrow night," he says and then turns back to leave, taking another step.

"I'll go with you," I tell him quickly. He only nods his head and keeps walking. I know he heard me, and I know where to find him when I finally get a grip on what the fuck is going on. I only have a few hours to figure something out. But I will.

It's only when I hear the faint click of the front door to the shop that I look down at the photo. I run my fingers down the creases to flatten it as best I can and take in the sight of a beautiful woman.

Her pale skin is complemented by the dark locks of her hair. I'm not sure where she is in the photo; it could be anywhere. The background is merely a brick wall as she looks off into the distance.

I don't know who she is, but she seems so familiar. The way she smiles, the look in her eyes, they strike something in me. A memory I don't have access to.

Jay's told me what happened when he was younger. The descriptions were so vivid I felt as if I was there. I run the tips of my fingers over her face, wondering if she's really the girl he talked about all those years ago.

I glance up at the empty doorway reluctant to believe Jay and to trust he's not going to hurt her. I can't help him do this, but I need to be there for her. I need to protect her. That one thought rings through my blood. I need to be there to help her. I need to get her away from Jay.

CHAPTER 3

Robin

Twenty years ago

*M*y head hurts so bad. Why does it hurt so much? I try to push myself upright, and the ground is so cold and hard. It's so uncomfortable, but my head is too heavy and I slump against the ground.

Where am I?

I try to remember where I was. The sound of the carousel shrieking as it slowly turned from the blowing wind filters through my memory. The empty swings sway back and forth. The school playground is deserted. I thought everyone would be here today. But it's empty. The first day of summer and not a soul is here.

I remember how I looked up and the sun was far off in the distance, but still in the sky. Didn't they know we still had time to play? I'm younger than most of the kids, only twelve, but even the older ones usually play with me.

I sat on the swings for a while. I remember that. As the

pounding in my head throbs harder I remember how the metal chains twisted and I let myself twirl on the swings over and over. I could wait for the other kids. I was sure they'd show up.

Did they?

I squint, trying to remember and I turn my head. My palms brush against the concrete floor, my cheek flat against the hard floor.

There was a man. He had a golf club and he needed my help. I remember how lost he looked. He said he hit his last ball into the trees and he couldn't reach into the bushes.

My heartbeat quickens as I remember, and my body goes still.

I knew to tell him a lie. I knew to turn around and run when he tried to take my hand in his. But he looked so hurt when I tried to pull away. He was genuinely upset, and all he did was ask me to help him.

The thin branches cracked under my sneakers as I went into the woods, following him to where he thought the ball had landed.

I open my eyes and I can't breathe.

He lied to me. My nails scratch on the ground as I clench them into fists and slowly look up.

No! Mommy, help me! Tears blur my vision of the cinder block walls.

No! This can't be happening. I pull my knees into my chest and try to stand.

Why does my head hurt so much?

"Are you okay?" a soft voice asks from behind me, encouraging me as I shuffle across the ground and push myself against the cold wall. It takes a moment for me to wipe my eyes and see him.

He's just a boy.

His knees are knobby and he's thin, but his shoulders are broad and he has a look about him that lets me know he's older than me. There's another look about him, too.

Sorrow and sadness cloud his eyes. Or maybe I just imagined it, because the moment my vision focuses, a hard expression stares back at me. He doesn't move from where he is, crouching only a few feet from me.

"Where am I?" I ask him quickly. I don't know where the words come from. I feel hot and cold, and I'm so confused. "I want to leave."

He huffs and shakes his head at me, pushing himself up from the ground where he was and takes a step toward me. He's taller than me. In that moment, he scares me.

"You can't leave," he says simply.

My face crumples, and I shake my head. "My mother will-"

"We're stuck here!" he yells at me, the anger in his voice making me flinch. He stares at the wall behind me, his eyes flickering to the floor then back to me. "We can't leave."

As I start to protest, I hear a loud rough bark outside. It's followed by a series of vicious barks that continue over and over. I whirl around and face the only window. It's small and rectangular, covered in filth and high up on the wall. There's barely any light coming through. Maybe there's a bush planted in front of it. I'm not sure, but at the very least I know there are dogs close.

"Don't try to run," the boy says behind me and again I turn to face him. Threats all around me, and it's my fault. It's all my fault. So stupid! I wrap my arms around my shoulders. "My mother-"

"Stop." The boy gives me the command, and I do. I stop

because I'm a good girl. I've always been a good girl, but look at where it's gotten me.

It's quiet for a while, and the boy takes another step closer to me. I don't move. I don't know what to do or where I am, but deep down inside I know this boy isn't going to hurt me. There's something about him. Something broken and scared and angry even, but it's pure.

"What's going to happen to us?" I ask him weakly.

"He won't touch you. It's not about you."

"What?" I don't understand. I'm so confused.

"He's using you." He looks past me, anger evident as he clenches his jaw. "It's about making me do what he wants. He knows I won't..." his voice drifts off, and the anger changes into something else. Something I can't see because he turns his back to me.

I reach out to him, grabbing his arm to keep him from leaving me, moving purely out of instinct. The touch feels like a spark. As if I've put my hand to a flame, but before I can even process it, he whips back around to face me, a scowl of anger on his face as he stares at me. "I won't let him hurt you like he does me. All you are is a tool for him to use against me."

He takes another step closer to me, and for the first time I really get a good look in his eyes. The intensity almost makes me scoot back, but then I'd be against the wall. Trapped and cornered.

He parts his lips to answer me, but no words come out. Time passes, and the only thing I can hear is my heartbeat as he stares at me. His eyes don't break from mine, and I'm too scared to look away.

"I'm sorry," he says flatly, but then he turns away as if the sentiment were genuine.

For some reason, just hearing those words breaks me. The tears fall and as I wipe them away, he looks at me with distaste. I half expect him to tell me to stop, but he doesn't.

I struggle to calm myself and somehow I do. Maybe it's because I don't really believe him. I don't believe it's hopeless. My mother will find me, and she'll make that man pay for what he's done. Both to me and to this boy. I know she will.

"What's your name?" I ask to keep him from leaving me as he turns. I lick my lips, tasting the salty tears and wiping my cheeks. I don't want to cry. I want to get out of here.

"J-" he starts to answer me, but we both whip around and face the door as it opens, silencing us and making me instinctively back away from it.

I grab onto the boy's arm and try to hide behind him. I don't know a thing about him and the look he gives me nearly makes me run from both him and the man stalking into the room, but I don't get the chance. The boy grips my wrist with his other hand and pulls me closer to him, my front to his back and my back to the wall. He keeps himself deliberately positioned in between me and the man.

It's only when I grab onto the boy, my small fingers digging into the rough denim of his jeans at his hip and my cheek pressed against his back, that he lets go of me.

The boy may scare me some, but the man terrifies me.

CHAPTER 4

Robin

This sabbatical was a mistake. I'm only hours into it, but I'm already feeling like I need to do something. Anything. I just can't sit here and not focus on work. It's what I've done since I was a child. It makes dealing with everything so much easier.

I pull the blanket tighter around me and toss the paperback novel onto my nightstand. I tried reading the first page at least four times. My eyes would travel along the lines, but not a word would register. I just can't focus. I can't relax.

I flick the switch to the lamp, turning it off and rub my tired eyes. I can't sleep either, but that's nothing new. My back cracks as I lie back down and try to stretch out my neck. It's sore and so are my shoulders, so I fluff the pillow and put my head back down only to be agitated by how hot the pillow is.

I'm just not comfortable. Not physically, not emotionally. And I don't think I should be. I deserve this.

I turn onto my side and then back onto my stomach, hugging the pillow close to me. I thought tonight I'd be haunted by the last session I had with Marie. I thought it would be her eyes I'd see that kept me from slipping into a much-needed sleep and letting the exhaustion take over. Instead, it's *his* eyes.

Red-rimmed and brimming with tears. They fall down his face and he doesn't acknowledge them, he just stares at me, whispering that he's sorry. He hadn't told me he was sorry other than the first day. But weeks later, my strong protector stared at me and it was all he could say. My chest tightens, and I remember how the fear weighed against me. *"I'm sorry," he whispered.*

I TRY NOT TO CRY. HE ALREADY FEELS GUILTY, BUT HE shouldn't. His father uses me to make the boy do things he doesn't want to. It's not fair to him. What's worse is that I want him to protect me. How selfish I am. I'm sickened by it, but the fear of his father keeps me quiet as the days pass.

As I swallow the spiked lump in my throat, twisting my fingers around each other and ignoring the emotions rushing through my blood, my eyes dart to the boy's arm. The bruises are already dark, and there's a large scratch on his forearm. The blood is so bright. Such a vivid color. I'll never forget.

"I'm sorry," he says and his voice cracks and this time he wipes the tears away with the back of his hand as he sniffles. I've never seen him like this. I shake my head with my eyes closed, ignoring how my heart squeezes and my body goes cold.

His father is going to come for me. He's going to put me in the cage instead of the boy.

My mother isn't coming. No one is. It's been weeks. I knew the day would come when I would have to leave this room. I always thought it would happen after the boy was taken. Every time I'm alone in here, I'm scared his father will come back and he won't be able to protect me anymore.

But he let the boy come back to me with the threat that when he returns, he'll be taking me for his test.

I can't help but let the tears fall as I wrap my arms around my chest and try to keep the sobs from ripping from my throat. I can't blame the boy. He's kept me safe for so long. But he didn't listen. He wouldn't obey his father, and now the monster is going to come for me.

"It's okay," I say weakly, although the way my voice croaks, I don't even know if he can understand me.

He grips my shoulders with both of his hands. It's a bruising force that snaps me out of the fear of what's to come and captures my full attention. He's so close to me, so intense as he stares into my eyes. I don't think he's ever touched me before. Not like this, not since the first day when he shielded me. He doesn't like it when I touch him either. Especially when he has bruises.

He shakes his head, his eyes staying on mine. "React quickly," he tells me, and his face scrunches and he holds back his own emotions, breathing deeply before looking back at me with remorse. "He stops it if you show how scared you are."

His eyes pierce mine and I can't help but nod my head, although I'm not sure what he's talking about. He's never told me what happens when he leaves. He's not the same when he comes back and he likes to be alone, so I give him that space. "Don't try to be brave and hide it. He'll only make it worse."

I stare at him, but I don't answer. I can't do this. I need to be strong and not make this harder for him, but I'm terrified.

"Robin!" the boy screams my name, demanding an answer and my obedience, but before I can say anything, the heavy metal door swings open.

MY EYES SNAP OPEN AND I STRUGGLE TO TAKE A BREATH, quickly sitting up and shoving the suffocating blanket off me. I take a ragged breath and reach up to my shoulders where he was touching me. I swear I can still feel his fingers digging into me.

He was just a boy, but he tried so hard to protect me. I pull my knees into my chest and rest my head on my knees, focusing on breathing. He didn't deserve the fate he was given.

I lick my dry lips, willing the memories to go away.

It's been so long since they've been this vivid. I know it's the guilt. I left him there. He took so much of the pain to try to save me. He's the only reason I could escape, and in return, I left him behind.

Small tears leak from the corners of my eyes, wetting my lashes and landing hard on my silk nightgown. I wipe them away and then reach for the bottle of pills on my nightstand.

I know I need to see someone for this. I can't keep taking pills just to sleep, just to keep the night terrors from surfacing, but I'm too ashamed to admit it all.

I'm too much of the coward that I was when I was a

child.

I take two pills, hoping they'll help. Last night they didn't. Hours passed and sleep didn't come. It only makes the mornings worse, but maybe tonight, it'll come. I swallow the now room temperature water and set the glass down on the nightstand.

My back and shoulders hurt as I roll over again. I bunch the blanket between my knees and shift on the mattress. It's the best money can buy, but it can't soothe my sore body. It can't lull me into a deep sleep that keeps the nightmares from surfacing.

Nothing can save me.

It's a weird feeling when you know you're about to fall asleep. Your body seems to go weightless for just a moment. My limbs turn numb and everything feels heavy. So heavy but like I'm floating, a sweet contradiction that tells me sleep is coming.

I'm conscious of it, fully aware a deep sleep within reach. And that's when the floor creaks and my body wakes instantly, tense and stiff.

I keep my eyes closed, too afraid to open them. My heart races in my chest, and I'm too scared to move. *Maybe it's all in my head*, I tell myself, but the second I do, I hear the floorboards creak again with the heavy weight of someone walking into my bedroom.

My back is to my nightstand, but I know my car alarm is there. My keys are sitting somewhere on it in the dark. I need to move, if for no reason than to make a disturbance. I suck in a breath as I roll my body over, not looking at whoever is here.

I don't care who it is, I'll fight them. I won't go down

easy and be a good little victim. I refuse to.

I knock the glass of water over, and it shatters on the floor. At the same time, the bed dips low with the weight of the intruder. I scream out as he grabs me, my fingers grasping at the ceramic cup that holds my keys, my earrings, my lip balm. The rim of the cup brushes along my fingertips as a rag covers my face.

I breathe in once, both of my hands reaching up toward my mouth. My fingers struggle to pry the large hand away, scratching as my muffled screams prove how useless my fight was.

His heavy leg lays over mine, pinning me down as I breathe in again.

Chloroform.

I can smell it, and it's then that I know I'm fucked.

I struggle until I can't.

I scream until my throat's raw.

And when my body finally goes heavy and numb again, that weightless feeling taking over, my eyes roll back and I catch a glimpse of the man.

His eyes.

So gray. Even in the dark of night, I know it's *him*. The sharp lines of his handsome face are different from those I remember. My hand reaches up, my fingers brushing his rough stubble before falling without my consent.

He's alive. I will my eyes to stay open for just a bit longer. Just to be sure he's real.

The boy's alive. My heart squeezes, and the realization is too much to bear. It shatters my sanity, my composure.

And then the darkness takes over in one slow wave, and all at once, I surrender myself to him.

CHAPTER 5

Robin

Twenty years ago

I'm so used to this room. I don't know how long it's been, but I don't bother to count the days anymore. I don't hope for Mama to come find me anymore. I know it's useless now, and it only makes me more upset.

The only solace I have is lying beside me. I speak without thinking, just saying what's on my mind to break up the silence in the cold room.

"I wish I were a bird." I blink at the faint light shining through the small window so high up on the cinder block wall. "Then I could fly away." My voice lowers to nearly a whisper and I turn on the hard ground, facing the boy at my side. I tuck my arm under my head and swallow the lump in my throat as I avoid his gaze. It's such a serious look in his light gray eyes. I can hardly stand the chill that runs through me.

Some days I think he's angry with me. I can't shake the

thought that he hates me; that he hates being stuck here with me, both of us helpless and at the hands of his heartless father.

"Both of us." I clear my throat and chance a look up at him as I add, "I mean I wish we were both birds." I turn to gesture toward the far wall as I explain, "So we could fly through that window."

The boy smiles at me, although I don't think it's genuine. "But it's closed," he says in a voice so rough and low it makes goosebumps spread across my skin. He clears his own throat, propping up his head in his hand and leaning on his elbow to look down at me. My heart does a weird flip in my chest, fluttering when he leans closer to me. I can feel the heat of his body. He's older than me. He looks it, too. I feel my cheeks heat with a blush and I look away, turning back to the window and pulling at the thin gown I have on. It's not enough to keep me warm down here and I know if I were just a bit closer to the boy, I'd be more comfortable, but I keep my distance.

"Well, what animal then?" I ask the boy, curling on my side and tucking both arms beneath my head.

He's quiet for a moment, but then he answers, "A wolf could break it."

I resist the urge to turn to face him, closing my eyes as they roll and a small smile forms on my lips. A wolf could never fit through that window.

I decide to play along, feeling a warmth run through me as I hear him scoot closer to me. He never touches me, but he likes to be close to me. And I like it too although I don't tell him. "Well, you be a wolf and break the window, and I'll be a bird. Together we can run away."

"I saw a wolf kill a bird once on TV," he says, but the boy's voice is devoid of emotion and the shock of what he said makes

me turn to face him, sitting up and pulling my knees into my chest.

"Why would a wolf do that?" I feel my brows pinch and my lips turn down; I know it's obvious I'm horrified from what he said, and it only makes him laugh.

He shrugs his shoulders and picks at a spot on the concrete floor, a satisfied smirk on his lips. Something about the look on his face makes my heart do that fluttering motion again and I find myself inching forward, my toes barely touching his thigh. But we both notice that they touch.

"A wolf doesn't have any reason to hurt a bird." I stare at him, but he still doesn't look up at me. "I don't understand."

The boy tilts his head to look at me and this time, the expression is something I've never seen before. There's a rawness in the light gray flecks, a heat on the outer edge where his eyes get darker. Almost like a flicker of a flame giving his gaze an intensity that makes my body freeze, but not with a coldness, with a burning heat.

"I think he did it," the boy starts to say, licking his lower lip and staring right through me, not caring that I can't even breathe when he looks at me like that, "I think he did it just because he wanted to."

CHAPTER 6

John

$\mathcal{I}$ pick at my thumbnail with my teeth as I stand in the corner of the dark room. I'm anxious, and adrenaline is pumping hard in my blood. Jay's a fucking bastard. He didn't tell me until it was already done.

I should go to the police and turn him in. I know that. Even as I pace in the small dark corner and stare at the woman on the bed, I know I should.

But I won't. Jay set me up. He said it was collateral, using my car and leaving evidence behind although he won't tell me what. I'm fucked. I grit my teeth remembering how he smiled at my anger.

I don't know what to do other than to keep her safe, but as the time ticks by I start to wonder if I'd do more harm than good. If being close and looking out for Jay would bite me in the ass. And in this case, the woman caught in Jay's gaze. I can't tell him no though. A low rumble in my throat pisses me off. I know Jay needs me and I'm fucked because I just can't walk away from him.

It reminds me of when we were kids. How I got along with everyone. A decent student and friendly by nature. Jay wouldn't come around to the playground often then. Very rarely. But some days I'd sit by the edge of the broken swing set, and he'd show up then. It scared me when he'd stay away for a long time. He wouldn't tell me where he went. All he'd say is that he wasn't wanted, but I shut that shit down. I wanted him around because I knew he needed someone. I could sense how desperate he was, but he was too afraid to open up. Too afraid to let anyone in. Except me, I guess.

The other kids didn't see him like I did. They mostly ignored him or, if they were honest with themselves, they were terrified to look him in the eye. That's the air around him that pushed everyone away. And the moment anyone would dare to approach us, Jay was gone. Uninterested in associating with anyone else. Despite all that, we got along just fine, better than fine most of the time. I knew how to be a good friend to him and he did the same for me when times got rough. We got close fast. Almost like brothers.

"Jay?" the woman calls out softly, and the sheets rustle as she turns onto her side, pulling her knees into her chest. Her voice is ragged, but not with fear, which is surprising. Just exhaustion. And it pulls me from my memories and back to the present.

She's even more gorgeous in person. I'm practically terrified to go any closer to her. She calls to me in a way I can't describe or justify. Her hair is a messy halo on the white pillow and her skin looks soft and smooth, so much of it exposed in the skimpy silk nightgown she's wearing. I only went to her to pull the thin sheet over her body, covering her curves although they're still prominent under the sheet.

"Robin?" I whisper her name and clear my throat when it comes out raspy. Jay's gone. He brought me here and left to get supplies. Things he said she'd need. I've never been to his home until now, but I couldn't have guessed for even a second it would be this nice.

He said it's for her. That it's always been for her, although he didn't know it until he was ready to take her. The way he talks about her has me on edge. He's obsessed, but only with healing her. Only in righting his sins.

All I know about her is her name, that she tried to kill herself, and that she has a past with Jay. He didn't give me anything else. He said she'd have to tell me.

"Jay?" the woman calls out again, her voice groggy as she rises on the mattress, bracing her arm behind her and slowly sitting up. She puts a hand on her forehead and lets out a small moan.

I hesitate only a moment more before taking three large strides closer before stopping at the foot of the bed. "You're safe," I tell her gently, raising my hands with my heart racing in my chest. "I promise I will keep you safe," I say and the words come out with strength. I will keep that promise if it's the last thing I do.

"Jay," she says softly, reverently almost and it shocks me. My brow pinches as I step closer to her, rounding the bed, but careful not to touch it. I don't even brush my knees against it. I don't want to give her any indication at all that I'll touch her.

"Jay went out," I tell her and try to breathe, I try to explain what's going on. "He wants to help you, and I'm here to make sure you're safe."

The small woman looks up and flinches. Her eyes go wide before she backs away slowly. So slowly it looks like the sheet barely moves as it falls down her body. She sucks in a breath and visibly swallows before I add, "I'm John."

"John?" she asks in a whisper before her eyes dart to the door and then back to me.

She's disoriented. The drugs are still coursing through her system, but the fear has finally set in.

"It's okay, I won't let Jay hurt you," I tell her, again raising my hands palms outward as though she's a wounded animal.

Her eyes fall to the sheet and then look back to me before she sits up to look at me, her gaze searching my face for something. She finally asks, "Does Jay want to hurt me?" Her eyes flicker to the door again and then back to my eyes.

The dim light in the room reflects in her eyes. Swirls of forest greens and flecks of gold. She has the most gorgeous eyes I've ever seen, but they're riddled with questions and fear.

"No," I answer her immediately. "He wants to help you."

She nods once and then the fear seems to dim although she unconsciously picks at the blanket on the bed.

63

"Are you alright?" I ask her, feeling deep down in the pit of my stomach that there's more between her and Jay than I realize. She's more afraid of me than him. I can feel it. "I promise, I have no intention of hurting you," I tell her and slow my movements to make it obvious I'm going to sit on the edge of the bed. I can't have her being afraid of me.

"I'm not well, no," she says softly, shaking her head just slightly but her eyes stay on mine, brimming with curiosity now. "Are you alright?" she asks me.

It throws me off. "No," I say after a moment. "This isn't alright with me," I add with my throat tight. "I didn't know," I explain, and I tell her more as a plea for forgiveness. I swallow hard and glance at the door. I should take her away. I can leave with her right now.

All the evidence will point to me though and if she presses charges, I'm fucked. But what other choice do I have?

"If you want to leave-" I start to say, but she cuts me off.

"What didn't you know?" she asks me, licking her lips and tilting her head to the right. Her eyes are wide with curiosity more than anything else.

"I didn't know he'd taken you," I admit to her in a low voice that's barely audible. She nods her head once.

"So you'd let me leave?" she asks in a small voice. Her eyes travel to the door as if watching herself simply walk away, but when her gaze stops, the lights turn on and Jay stands in the doorway. My eyes adjust to the light slowly, but they only focus on her and her reaction to seeing Jay.

She hesitates a moment, her grip on the blanket tightening as she takes him in.

"Jay?" She whispers his name as if it's a question. As if it can't really be him.

My gaze turns to Jay, and I watch as his lips twitch up into a smile and his expression softens. He opens his mouth to say something, but instead he licks his lips and reaches behind him to close the door. A foreboding click echoes off the walls as he walks closer to her.

"How's your head?" he asks her.

"Jay, are you alright?" she asks and then crawls to the edge of the bed slowly, moving away from me and closer to him. Her eyes brim with tears, and she bites down on her bottom lip to keep them from spilling over.

He walks slowly toward her, and the sound of his boots smacking softly on the wooden floor is the only thing I can hear other than my racing heart.

He cups her chin in his hand and brushes his thumb along her lips, and she seems to lean into him. She reaches up and wraps her small hands around his wrist. "I know it's scary, but I thought you'd understand."

"You can't do this, Jay," she pleads with him as a tear slips down her cheek. The way she's talking to him, the way she pleads with him and ignores me completely shifts something deep inside of me. *She cares for him.* It's so fucking obvious.

"It's not just for me, little bird," Jay says in a pained voice. "I would have left you alone forever, I promise you I would have."

She shakes her head, rising on her knees to interrupt

him. As the bed creaks with her shifting weight, he presses a finger to her lips, hushing her. "You wanted to hurt yourself," he tells her and her strength vanishes. She moves her cheek from his hand and seems to back away from him.

"Jay, you need help," she whimpers.

"Ah," Jay says. "And so do you, my little bird."

CHAPTER 7

Robin

I'm practically shaking. My legs feel wobbly and my head is pounding, but I've never felt so aware.

It's him. It's really him. After all this time, he's finally come back to me. But this is a nightmare even I never dared to have. An outcome I couldn't have predicted.

"You're broken, Robin," Jay says and his voice breaks my thoughts. I stare at him, his eyes never looking so cold and his voice never feeling so devoid of emotion before. But he's right here in front of me. His jawline sharper, his shoulders broader and his body filled out.

He's no longer a scared little boy trying to protect me. He's become a man in every way.

"Why did you do it?" he asks me, and my blood turns to ice. I flinch as the memory comes back full force. The cold wind whipping across my face, the branches lashing out and striking me as I ran through the forest. I ran because I had no choice. *Liar!* a voice hisses in the back of my head. I didn't have to leave him behind. I'm a coward. I ran because I was scared.

"Why did you try to kill yourself?" Jay asks me and my eyes lift to his, my heart still hammering in my chest.

My throat feels dry and my voice comes out hoarse, but I'm grateful I misunderstood. I'm grateful he doesn't bring it up. I wish I could go back; I wish I could pretend I never left him. "I'm not well, but I'm-" I try to explain, but he cuts me off.

"Broken!" Jay yells at me, and for the first time real fear flows through me.

"I'm sorry I left you," I say. The words spill from me unbidden and I cover my mouth, hating that I've acknowledged it. I look up to him, watching for his reaction. But I get nothing, not a word or any recognition. "Please, don't hate me," I whimper. I feel so small beneath him.

Maybe this is what I've truly wanted. For him to punish me. For him to forgive me.

His large hand pats the back of my head, a comforting touch that brings me back to the first night I met him. When I lay on the ground crying until he finally reached out to comfort me.

"Don't be sorry," he says. "This isn't about that. It has nothing to do with how we left. It's only about who we've become since then."

"Why are you doing this?" I ask him. "You know it doesn't have to be like this," I say and my eyes search his, pleading and begging. "You didn't have to do this." My voice comes out as a hollow whisper.

"I did though," he tells me. "You have no idea what it's like. For me to know and be aware, and he… he doesn't. He doesn't see it."

I shake my head, grabbing onto the edge of the bed and the comforter as I insist, "That's not how this works, Jay!" I try desperately to get through to him. For him to understand. "I can't help you like this."

He breathes in heavy, and his eyes pierce into me for a long moment, like he's considering what I'm telling him. But eventually he nods his head. "Yes, you can. And I can help you," he says.

The hot tears flow freely now. "Jay, please," I beg him. My head starts to spin, and I feel faint. This can't be happening.

"You're going to stay here until we can help each other. Until you forgive me, and I forgive you."

It's like a spike to the heart to hear him talk of forgiveness. "I never blamed you," I say, telling him the truth. I never once blamed Jay for any of the fucked up shit that happened to us. "I hated myself for leaving you. And now-" my voice cracks realizing what he's become and how fucked up this all is. I should never have left him.

"You need help," I plead with him again, my voice wretched. I wipe the tears away with the back of my hand as I remember John. How he looked at me as if he'd never seen me before in his life.

"I know," he replies and his voice is raw and his eyes go glassy, but his expression is hard. "You can help me, and I can help you." He tilts his head, and it pains my heart.

My heart tries to leap up my throat. I feel sick as my stomach churns.

"This is your new home for a little while," he says. My heart squeezes in my chest, and I reach up to cling to Jay's shirt.

"Jay, no!" I cry out as he grips my hands in his and keeps me from holding onto him. I try to move toward him, to beg him to let me go. My nails scrape along his wrists. "Jay!" My pleas are useless.

"You don't have to do this," I urge as he backs away and I nearly fall off the bed. My eyes search frantically for the door and the moment they do; Jay squeezes my hands tighter. He squeezes hard enough so there's pain, but for only a moment and my eyes shoot to his.

My heart thuds in my chest, and the blood drains from my face. "Don't do this," I whisper, but my words fall on deaf ears. Jay turns his back on me and I scramble off the bed, but he's through the door and slamming it shut just a moment before I can reach him.

"No!" I scream at him, pounding my fists against the door. *Bang! Bang!* "Don't leave me in here!" I cry out for Jay as tears stream down my face and my voice goes raw. "Jay!"

Bang! Bang! I don't stop screaming; I don't stop pounding.

For so long I've dreamed of him coming back for me. I prayed he'd be safe.

If only I'd known.

I turn my back to the door, leaning against it as I slowly slide to the floor. My shoulders hunch and I feel useless, hopeless… worst of all, like a child again.

Yes, that's exactly how I feel. Like I'm back in the past

all those years ago. But back then, Jay was my shoulder to cry on. My protector. *My savior.*

Now, I'm truly alone.

John. I hear him say his name in the depths of my memory, I see the look in his eyes and my own pop open.

He'll come back at some point. And hopefully sooner, rather than later.

John will come back, and I can use him. Tears prick my eyes, and my throat closes with emotion. I can't do that to him. I'm consumed by guilt. I can't stop having flashbacks of me running away.

But I have to try. Jay's not well, and I have to get him help. He's not okay, and I can't just stay here waiting around. Not for Jay, and not for John. I need to get the fuck out of here.

CHAPTER 8

Robin

I open my eyes slowly; the light is still harsh, and my head's groggy. The chill is starting to get to me, and I've only just now realized I'm still in my thin silk nightgown.

That fucking bastard. I clench my hands into fists and grind my teeth as I try to comprehend what's happened.

He's alive. Jay is alive.

That little bit of knowledge in and of itself is earth shattering to me. My head falls back against the door and my throat feels tight. My heart aches for him.

I struggle to breathe as I push up from the floor and lean against the door to stand. My eyes slowly focus on the room he's put me in, and it feels like a spike to my chest. A sob tries to escape, but I push it down, swallowing it and refusing to cry.

It looks the same as before... like a deliberate attempt to bring me back.

I shake my head. No, this isn't the same. "It can't be." The words creep through my lips as my shoulders quiver.

Cinder block walls yes, but the wall with the door is drywall. I blink the tears back, my eyes going glassy as I turn to face it and then the bed. It only has a simple frame with a mattress covered by a white fitted sheet and a thin white sheet on top. Only one pillow is on the bed, also white and still rumpled from where I was lying.

There was never a bed before. Was there? I don't remember one.

No, that's something I would remember. I'm sure of it. I lay on the ground next to him with a tattered blanket. Instinctively I look for the blanket, as if it'll be crumpled in a corner. The far right corner, the one farthest from the door. The one where we used to huddle together.

I swallow thickly, brushing my eyes with the back of my hand.

This room is made to look the same, but it's not.

That house was burnt down. I remember the smell. The ashes. I remember the fear that he was in there when it happened. That the boy had died, and was burned alive. I wanted to die myself. I screamed, and the officer held me close until my mother came to me.

She was crying, too. Even as she held me firmly against her chest, my tears soaked her shirt and hers fell into my hair.

The knowledge that there was no one inside didn't take the pain away. A pain that's never left me, a pain that's enough to render me useless in this moment.

My eyes feel heavy as I turn to the door again. It doesn't look like the old door. It was steel and gray. It was a door that couldn't be broken down. This one is painted white with a simple handle. No locks.

"No locks," I whisper and lick my dry lips.

I reach a hand out and then look up toward the ceiling. The far right is where the camera was all those years ago. I make a full circle, the sound of my feet shuffling across the floor accompanies me as I search for cameras in the room. But there are none.

Is he not watching? I find it hard to believe. I don't understand. A throbbing pulse makes me wince and I close my eyes until it goes away, holding both of my hands to the sides of my head.

What are you doing, Jay?

Why this? I open my eyes, remembering John. Maybe he convinced him? It hurts to think that way. It fucking shreds me, but it fuels me to move. I need to get out. I'm not safe here, and neither is he.

I grip the doorknob, expecting it to be locked, but it's not. My heart stutters and I test it again.

It's too easy. I jiggle the knob again, and it turns easily. The soft click fills the air as I turn it and pull the door open slowly.

I can't breathe. My heartbeat is too fucking loud.

I stand in the open doorway, too afraid to peek out, but somehow I force myself.

My brow knits as I rest my hand against the doorjamb and bite down on my lip, looking down a hall to what appears to be a basement. There's a door at the very end, faint morning light spilling in and a set of stairs leading up to the outdoors.

I cautiously take one step, my bare foot sliding across the cement.

Did he really just forget to lock the door? Or is this a test?

I don't take a moment to think. I don't try to understand.

He's not well, and he needs help, desperately. I can get him help. The thought pushes me to move faster, one step at a time as I look over my shoulder to a set of stairs that leads to the first floor of this house. I can't hear a damn thing other than the blood pounding in my ears and the slamming of my heart.

My palms turn sweaty as I keep walking.

I can leave and get help. I'll come back for him.

My body buckles at the thought, and I lean against the door to my potential freedom. The doorknob is cold in my hand.

I was going to come back, I almost whisper. I tried. I tried to go back, but the house was gone. I close my eyes, my body trembling and the memories flooding my mind.

His eyes are the same. God, his eyes are everything. The only thing I can see. The boy and the man looking at me are the same.

He needs help. I need to help him.

A low growl makes my body tense. It continues, long and low and threatening, and coming from my right.

I can't breathe remembering the dogs. No. No. I'm frantic as I rip the door open, pulling with everything I have and luckily, it too swings open and doesn't hold me back.

75

It bangs hard against the wall, the harsh noise joining with the loud bark of the dog. I can't help but look back, and staring straight at me are the dark eyes of a large black dog. His hackles are raised. He's snarling and his white teeth are exposed, drool dripping from his jowls as he snaps them shut and barks again repeating his vicious warning.

My legs seem frozen, yet they move me forward. Terrified and without any other option, I move so quickly my body slams into the concrete wall straight ahead.

I reach back to the door, my hand slipping on the metal doorknob as terror races through my blood.

I try to close the door, I try to lock him in the house and escape, but it's too late. The dog is too close. He charges for me. His large muscular body propels him at a speed I can't match. A scream is ripped from my throat as I take the stairs two at a time.

The dog's teeth clamp down on my legs near the top of the stairs and I fall hard, landing on my side with half my body still on the cement stairs and the upper half laying in a mixture of mud and grass. The dog releases me in an instant, but the moment I move my legs, a rough and vicious snarl rips through the air.

Jay.

My heart shatters in my chest.

His father had dogs too. How could he? How could he do this to me?

I try to get to my knees, to make a feeble attempt to run, but the black dog snarls and bites down on my arm the moment I lift it. He's so close, so massive. He must be ninety, or maybe a hundred pounds and built with speed and muscle.

I'm no match for him. My cheek rests on the grass as my body stills. I'm frozen with fear. The dog doesn't bite down, and he doesn't growl, he merely holds me in place.

Waiting for his owner.

The dog's teeth feel so sharp as I whimper. My body's shaking, freezing in the cold dirt and earth at the bottom of the cement stairs. The early morning sun rises, and it's enough light that I can see around me. Trees, open land… nothing else. Nowhere to go, no one to call for help.

Just like before. *He's dead.* I have to remind myself. The monster is dead. He didn't burn in the fire, but he was there, buried in the dirt.

It's just Jay. He's the one doing all this.

I pray that it's him. I pray for him to come to me and make this all go away. Make the memories go away.

The most fucked up part about it all, is that I don't hate him. I wish I could find it in me to focus on that strong emotion, but it's absent.

Even as fear cripples me and the sound of the dog's low growling vibrates up his chest and into my small body… I can't manage hate.

The sound of a man's strides makes me open my eyes. I force them to look back at the man walking toward me. His hands are fisted, his jaw clenched and a disapproving frown is on his face.

A low whistle pierces through the air, and the dog's jaws loosen before he backs away.

I still don't move. I lie there, my knees on the cement and the scratches from the dog bite burning and begging me to touch them. But I don't. I just stay there listening to the man approaching. I close my eyes as he nears, hating everything that's happening. Hating my failure, the circumstances. Hating everything but him.

He can drag me back inside; I won't fight him. I never could before anyway.

My eyes are too dry to cry, but that doesn't stop the guilt that smothers me when I peek up, his shadow blocking the light and I see the look of betrayal in his eyes.

CHAPTER 9

Jay

I knew she'd do it. I remind myself of that as I carry her back down the stairs.

She's so light in my arms. Her small body is hot and she clings to me as if she didn't just try to run from me. Her hot breath tickles my neck as she nestles her head there and stays still in my arms. She won't look at me though.

And for some reason that makes me feel justified.

It shouldn't though. I practically set her up for this, but it doesn't make it hurt any less.

I climb down the cement stairwell to the opened door and whistle for Toby to come in. He's a German shepherd I picked up after his partner, a police officer, died on the job. He was shot in the back and the fuckers got Toby, too.

He barrels in, taking glances at Robin, my little bird. He's curious but he'll stay away. I trained him well, and he knows how to behave and what to do.

"Good boy," I mutter under my breath as his paws patter in the basement and I kick the door shut. I think about locking it, but there's no point.

Robin sniffles and readjusts in my arms, but she's quiet. Her face is filthy, with a large smudge of dirt on her cheek, but she doesn't even try to wipe it away.

"I have a room for you upstairs, you know," I tell her as I walk her back to the room. It's just like where I first met her. Just like the room we spent months and months in.

She finally looks at me, those beautiful hazel eyes brimming with curiosity. With hope.

"It was your reward for being good for me. All you had to do was stay." Her eyes flick down and her body tenses as I push my back against the door to the room and walk her to the bed.

"I'm sorry, Jay," she whispers in a cracked voice. The light in here is bright. It's not like the one Father had. That one was dim and dirty, covered with filth that had gathered for years. This light is new. It's too glaring.

"You aren't though," I tell her as I set her down on the bed. I brush the sheets with my arm and look at her dirtied nightgown and the scratches on her leg from Toby. There's a trickle of blood on her calf and I'm almost proud that Robin stays still when I grab her just beneath her knee to look at it.

"He got you, didn't he?" The words slip out before I know it. I hate that he hurt her. Anger makes my body feel tight, my corded muscles ready to spring to life.

But it's not his fault. He was merely doing what he's been trained to do. As if hearing my thoughts, he whines from just beyond the closed door. My head turns to it, and I bite back the rage. It's not his fault she ran.

"I'm sorry, I really am." I look back at Robin, watching her pale lips part and then tremble as she waits for me to respond. Her eyes look everywhere but into mine.

"Scared little bird, aren't you?"

"Jay, you need help," she tells me again, her words a broken whisper. I nod my head in agreement though. My mind is fucked up, splintered and it hurts. It literally fucking hurts.

"I know," I whisper back.

"I can take you to the hospital…" my sweet little Robin says, as if that's the answer. As if there's a cure for this. There's not. I've already tried. I can't be like this anymore. The only cure for me is her.

I try to blink away the memories of the nurse holding me down to the bed. How they had to tie me down. I had to behave so they'd let me go. I had to hide who I was, and what I'd done. But with her, I won't have to hide.

"I won't go back there," I say and grit my teeth, my body tensing. "I'm not going anywhere, Robin."

"Let me go," she pleads with me, but that's quite the opposite of what I'll be doing.

I shake my head once and reach into my back pocket, my fingers slipping around cool metal. The handcuffs click as I pull them out for her to see, and she dares to back away from me.

I snatch her ankle and yank her back toward me. Her fingernails scrape along the bed and she arches her back instinctively, but she lets me drag her close. It's so tempting, the desire to push her obedience. I hover over her, my dick hardening and my breathing coming in heavy.

"Jay, please," she whimpers with her eyes closed, her chest rising and falling.

"This wouldn't be necessary if you hadn't tried to leave me again," I tell her and my own heart squeezes with pain as her face crumples and she lets out a sob. "I'm sorry," she tries to say again, but it's a silent statement.

I feel bad for her, I really do, but it doesn't make the anger wane. Not in the least.

"I've waited so long," I confess to her. I lower my head to rest on her chest, feeling the dirty silk against my forehead and breathing in her sweet scent. It fills my lungs as my hands reach up and grip the bed on each side of her hips.

I've watched her almost every day. Well, night. The knowledge that I have to wait makes me even madder. I can only see her at night. But every chance I got to make sure she was okay, I took. I had to; there's a deep-seated need within me to ensure she's okay.

She's mine to protect. Mine to keep safe.

Yet she tried to hurt herself. "I knew you needed me," I whisper against her skin and lift my head to look at her. Her lips are parted as she breathes, her hair a tangled mess against the white sheets.

I catch a glimpse at a smudge of dirt on the white sheet and my blunt fingernails dig into the mattress.

"This needs to come off," I grunt through my clenched teeth, rising and gripping her nightgown in both hands. The handcuffs fall to the floor with a loud thud as she writhes under me.

"Jay!" she cries out my name, struggling to keep me from removing her filthy gown.

I let her arms flail, I let her nails scratch down my forearms, but I rip the thin silk fabric easily. It needs to come off of her. The memory of watching her lie on the dirty ground meshes with the sight of her running just now. I blink and there's a child in front of me; I blink again and it's her today.

My body sways as the memories taunt me. She left me. She didn't have to today. She didn't have to leave me again!

My body bristles with fury as I tear at the silk.

"Jay, please," she whimpers and backs away from me as I rip the muddy fabric from her and throw it onto the cement floor. She scuttles away from me until her back hits the wall. "Jay, no!" she screams.

The look in her eyes is what stops me. She's fucking terrified.

My body shakes as I calm my breathing. I blink again and again. My hands clench and unclench, and I stand there paralyzed.

A moment passes, and then another. I stare as Robin watches me cautiously and I wonder if John's here, but I know he's not. He'll come back in the morning. *It's just us.* I close my eyes and rest my knee on the bed, hanging my head low and hating that I've scared her.

"I-" I try to talk to her, to apologize and calm myself. "I need to clean you," I tell her although I speak with my head down and then raise my head to look her in the eyes. "You need your things," I say and try to sound sane. I know I'm crazy, I know I'm fucked in the head. But I'll never hurt her. I don't want to, anyway. "I'm sorry," I whisper and crawl onto the bed, slowly and making sure she knows I'm here for her. She tries to cover herself with her hands, and my blood heats with both shame and desire.

I grip the sheet, fisting it, I drag it up to her until she takes it.

I don't stop moving, and even as she tries to wrap the sheet tightly around her body, I lie close to her, like I used to.

"Jay," she says softly as I lie beside her and rest my head on the pillow. "I'm scared."

I nod my head, acknowledging her admission and knowing she has reason to be scared. It fucking hurts. I wish I wasn't like this. I wish I could have come to her and helped her without this fucked up head of mine. I close my eyes and wait for her to relax. She always did. Always. It didn't matter how bad the day was, or what had happened. Even the day he took her.

She let me hold her, and eventually she'd relax in my arms and fall asleep. *Always.*

I count the time, using her breaths as a measure. Slowly she molds her body to mine. Slowly her breathing steadies. It will come back to her. It never left me. Not a single day has passed where I don't imagine her in my arms. Some nights I swear I still felt her warmth, but feeling her now, I know I was a fool.

"Jay, talk to me," she says softly. She always wanted to talk. I run my nose along her hair and when I let out a heavy sigh, feeling the weight of so many sleepless nights come down on me, her hair brushes against my nose, lifting with my hot breath.

"I don't want to live like this, Robin," I tell her and each word scratches its way up my throat. I feel my walls break. She's powerful like that. Only her. *I'm so fucking weak for her.*

"Please help me," I beg her as my eyes sting. She was made for me. I knew it all those years ago; I knew she was sent to me for a purpose.

"I need you," I whisper against the pillow, my hot breath mingling with hers. I close my eyes as she reaches up and sets her hand down ever so slowly on the side of my face. Her soft skin moves along my rough stubble, and I open my eyes to find hers on me.

"For John?" Her eyes search mine as she asks, and it makes me feel weak. A pathetic huff leaves me as I swallow and stare at the ceiling. It's not like it was back at the old house. The home I grew up in. Or basement, rather.

"John has no idea." I turn to her and add, "He doesn't want to…" I can't finish. I can't talk about it. This is why I need her. I wrap my arms tighter around her and pull her in close. I shut my eyes, just for a moment.

She'll heal me, and I'll heal her. I swear I will.

I just have to be careful. My little bird is so easily broken.

My eyes snap open and I tell her, "You need to listen to me, Robin." My voice gets tight. "Even if you don't forgive me. Even if you want to leave me, you must listen."

Robin rises, propping herself up on her elbow and

coming closer to me, holding me and lifting my chin so I'll look her in the eyes.

She shakes her head slightly, and I almost lose it. The anger is so close to the surface. It's always there, brimming just beneath my skin. "I forgive you," she whispers and keeps my gaze. "You never had to be sorry," she says but chokes on her words and with that I reach my arm up and pull her closer to me. She hangs her head low and I shush her again.

I rock her gently, thinking about how she looks at me like I can do no wrong. Like I'm broken and in need of fixing.

The thought used to make me hate her. I fucking hated being stuck with someone who gave me so much sympathy. I hated her for leaving. I hated how she had a normal life. How she wasn't fucked in the head like I was.

It wasn't until the sleeping pills that I realized. It wasn't until I heard her whispering my name in her sleep that I knew I had to take her back.

It was then that I saw things so clearly.

"Shh, Robin," I whisper as I rock her. "It's okay," I tell her even though I know it's not in the least.

Nothing is okay. Far from it.

CHAPTER 10

Robin

I've never been a good sleeper. Not that I can remember, anyway. My mother told me that I used to sleep like the dead. Once I fell from the sofa and my father grabbed me by the ankle and kept me from hitting my head. I just dangled there, fast asleep and completely unaware.

Of course that all changed when I was taken.

It's been years since I've fallen into a deep sleep and felt rested. Years since I've felt safe and able to sleep at ease.

Yet while I held Jay and let him hold me, it was so easy. So easy to drift into sleep. Maybe it's the drugs or the exhaustion… or maybe the weight of the guilt settling.

Only the guilty sleep in prison, and that's quite like what this is. I deserve to be here, because it's my job to heal him. I know it with everything in me.

He's broken because of me.

I roll slightly, feeling Jay's warmth cocoon me and slowly bring my hand to his chest. I never touched him back then, since he didn't like it. He'd always wake up, and I didn't want that. He needed rest more than I did. His gray Henley is unbuttoned at the top, and his broad muscular shoulders make the thin fabric pull tight.

I love his eyes; I always have even as they haunted me, but with them closed now I can focus on the small details of his face. How thick his lashes are, the rough stubble along his sharp jaw. The way his hair is short, but long enough to be messy.

A sad smile slips across my lips as I rest my fingers against his chest.

I wish I hadn't though, because he wakes instantly, gripping my wrist and making me gasp. His eyes pop open and the pale gray swirls in his eyes are full of emotion. He swallows visibly and with unease before letting go of my wrist.

He blinks the sleep from his eyes and turns to look over his shoulder, the bed creaking as he looks at the door and then back to me.

He wraps his heavy arm around me, pulling me closer to him so my body touches his and then shuts his eyes as if he's going back to sleep.

"Jay?" I whisper his name. I don't know what time it is, but it must be very early or very late.

"Robin," he says my name low, the deep rumble of his voice making the word linger between us.

"Let me touch you?" I try to be strong in my words, but they're weak. I've always been weak for him.

He stays still, but the moment I reach forward he grabs

my wrist out of instinct. His blunt nails dig into my wrist. My breathing stalls and I stare at where he holds me, giving him a moment. "You want me here to help you," I finally say and look up into his eyes. He's staring at my wrist as well, at his fingers curled and gripping with a force that's unbreakable. I can feel the blood pulsing; his grip is so tight.

I swallow and add, "You need to let me do whatever I can to help you." My voice quivers, and I have to look away. It's selfish of me. So fucking selfish. I want to touch him, simply because I want to. So many nights he's held me. He's let me rest my cheek against his shoulder, and my lips have even rested against his chest. But never my hands. My hands need to be down.

"Tomorrow," Jay finally says and releases me, leaving my hand dangling awkwardly in the air until I submit and lower it to the bed.

Jay lies still, with no indication he's going to handcuff me to the bed. And I almost swallow my words, the plea for him not to. I don't want to remind him, but I need reassurance.

My lips part, but the words don't come out.

"What is it?" he asks me in a no no-nonsense voice.

"I don't want you to handcuff me," I tell him quickly. He lies still, with no reaction and my nerves get the better of me. I peek up at him through my lashes. His face is like stone, emotionless even. "Jay, please," I beg him. My fingers itch to reach up and touch him, but I can't, so instead my fingernails dig into the comforter.

"You can't leave me," Jay says as if it's the only truth he knows.

This is wrong. He's not okay, and I'm not safe. But the two of us were never meant to be right.

I can't help what being with him does to me. I wish I could justify my feelings, but I know it's fucked up on too many levels.

All the feelings I have for him are hovering just below the fear.

The need to cling to him to stay safe is strong. It's hard to fight the urge to touch him. What's worse is that I don't want to keep myself from touching him.

"Go to sleep, Robin," Jay tells me, his large hand splaying along my hip as he adjusts me next to him like we used to lay, calming me and kissing the crook of my neck.

His rough stubble brushes along my sensitive skin, and my body bows to him. I can't deny the effect he has on my body. I can't help how I want him. I try to override my body's reaction to him.

"We need to talk," I try to tell him, but he shushes me. And I obey. Whatever fate Jay gives me, I'll take it. I know that with every piece of my being in this moment. I only exist because of him, and I'm guilty of a far worse crime than any he could commit against me. I'll bend to his will; I owe him that. *I owe him everything.*

"Go back to sleep," he tells me in an even voice. And for the first time in years, I do just that. I slip easily into the darkness and fall into the depths of a dream I once had long ago.

CHAPTER 11

John

The camera's set up and focused on her. She's sitting on the bed with her knees pulled into her chest. There's a room upstairs full of clothes for her, yet she's wearing a white t-shirt that's far too large for her and a pair of men's blue flannel pajama pants. Something Jay must have left for her to wear. She's alone on a tiny ass mattress with nothing else in the room except a metal chair.

I let out a tortured breath and drag the chair across the room. The metal legs scrape on the cement floor, and the screeching only pisses me off. Rubbing the sleep from my eyes, I think about how I've canceled everything to be here. It's like an obsession, picking at the back of my brain, the anxiety making my body tremble. But more than that, I'm curious.

I don't know what exactly happened between them,

but the way she looks at him and vice versa... I'm more than curious.

"How do you know Jay?" Robin asks me with her gaze still fixed on the sheet she's balling up in her hand. She dares to lift those hazel eyes to me, and I take a moment to consider what I want to tell her.

"We met when we were kids," I answer. I finally sit down a few feet away from the bed, but inside of the camera's field. I swallow thickly. "He helped me," I admit to her.

She picks at the sheet, but doesn't look down. Tilting her head, she asks me, "Helped you with what?"

"I was adopted and it was hard for me, but Jay was," I pause and clear my throat, remembering back to when we were kids. Both of us lost and feeling alone, feeling abandoned. "Jay was a good friend when I needed one." I nod my head once and then look back at her, but I have to rip my eyes away. It doesn't justify this.

"I see," Robin says softly and it reminds me that she's a shrink. A huff of a humorless laugh spills from my lips. "Are you analyzing me, Doctor Everly?" I ask her with humor in my voice, but she nods her head once.

"I hope you don't mind," she says in a soft voice, still picking at the sheet.

I try to swallow the spiked ball that's formed in my throat, but I can't. Instead I just talk. "I didn't want to do this," I tell her. "I'm afraid to not be here though." I look her in the eyes when I say, "When I came back here this morning, I was scared that I'd find-"

I shake my head, unable to continue. It makes me less of a man to leave. Less of a man to leave Jay with her. But there's something I don't know. It's like it's right in front of my face, something I know deep down inside that says it's all okay, that this is meant to happen like this.

"Jay doesn't want to hurt me," Robin says confidently, but then adds, "Maybe a small piece of him wants to. But I don't think he would."

I stare at her with wonder and ask, "Why would you give him the chance?" Her eyes narrow with pain and gloss over before she reaches farther onto the bed and pulls the sheets up to get comfortable.

"What do you know about me?" she asks me.

"You're a psychiatrist," I answer her. I almost add that I looked her up while she slept. That I know where she went to school and other details I was able to find online, but I shut my mouth. She's already frightened, and I'm holding on by a thread. "Did you want to become a shrink because of what… what you went through?" I ask her. My heart aches for her as I search her eyes for answers.

I've felt bad for Jay for so many years. It's why I could never leave his side. And I feel the same for her. Unabashedly so.

She shakes her head, her hair swishing over her shoulders as she looks past me and crosses her legs. She rocks slightly and says, "I wanted to go into law and make a difference, you know?" Her eyes find mine as her voice carries through the room.

"Law?" I nod my head and say, "I could understand that. I could see why you'd want to go that route."

I can see the red blinking light of the camera reflected in her eyes as she stares at it for a moment, and then she licks her lips and looks back at me.

"I used to think that the worst thing you could see before you die was the eyes of your killer," she tells me in a tone that's chilling. "And I wanted to stop that."

I take in an uneasy breath, rubbing the back of my neck and trying to ignore all the things Jay's told me of his past. They almost feel real as the images flash before my eyes.

"But it's not," she whispers.

I turn to look at her, my hand stilling on my neck and then slowly moving to my lap.

"Now I think the worst thing would be to see someone running away, someone ignoring your screams. Someone who could help you, but didn't." Her eyes tear up again, and she shudders.

"I don't think I could handle facing that," she says and waits for me to respond.

I fail to find the right words to tell her. I know it hurt Jay, because he's told me about the girl over and over.

"What else?"

"What else?" I ask her for clarification.

"What else do you know about me?" she asks.

"I know you were with him," I tell her, my blood chilling at the memories. "You were with him for a little while."

"For four months," she says and her voice cracks. She swallows and brushes a strand of hair from her face. "Two days over, actually," she says and smiles sadly. "I left him then," she says but chokes on her words.

"It's not your fault," I tell her honestly. I can feel the emotions from her. The disappointment and regret. "Anyone would have run," I add.

94

She nods, but her expression only turns more painful.

"So now you know why I'm doing this. But why are you?"

"I don't trust him," I tell her firmly. Surprisingly she simply nods, as if that's a given.

"So he's just a friend that you owe. Someone who's helped you, someone who's broken and fucked up and you feel like you need to help him to make sure he doesn't hurt me?"

I nod once at her analysis of the situation. My chest feels tight, and I hate how I feel restrained and like a damaged man for giving him this.

"Yes," I tell her and scratch the back of my neck as I consider how to word my next question right, but she cuts me off.

"What do you think of me?" she asks me, and it catches me off guard.

"What do you mean?"

She chews the inside of her cheek for a moment. "You know what happened." Her eyes dart to the door at the sound of Toby laying against it and making the door thud. "You know that I'm…" She doesn't finish, and instead she looks me right in the eyes and asks, "Do you think I'm crazy?"

My heart thuds in my chest, and I hesitate to answer. "I don't know everything-" I try to finish, but she cuts me off.

"Yes you do," she says quickly in a whisper. "I'll tell you a secret, John. No one left that house with a sound mind."

CHAPTER 12

Robin

I don't know what's more disturbing, talking to John about what happened in the past, or staring back at the blinking red light. It's just like the cameras that were in the ceiling. The ones that watched us in our room.

"You gave it to him?" I ask Jay, and he peeks over his shoulder as he continues to lead me up the stairs from the basement to the main floor.

"Gave him what?" he asks me. I tighten my hand on his as the wooden stairs creak. "The camera," I reply, and the answer itself makes my heart hurt. My body tenses and I try not to close my eyes because I don't want to see it.

'I thought it would help," Jay says as if it's not fucked up.

He opens the door at the top of the stairs and warm light floods my vision for a moment.

"The room, the dog, the camera...," I say without

thinking and pull my hand from Jay's to rub my eyes. When I pull my hand away, he's staring at me, a look of worry on his face. "It's not okay, Jay," I whisper.

"It's a second chance, little bird."

He shifts from side to side, but his body is tense. "You don't know what it's been like," he says in a tight voice, the anger coming through. "I'm trying, but some things need to be shown to him," Jay says, and my throat constricts at the thought of John.

"Jay," I speak softly, reaching my hand out to his, but he turns away and runs a hand through his hair. "Please listen."

"We do it my way first," he says, pushing the words through his teeth, his piercing eyes shining into mine and narrowed with authority.

"What if it makes it worse?" I ask him. He's playing with fire. I can already feel the creeping heat threatening to consume us both.

He licks his lips and takes my hand in his, looking past me as he says, "We're going to be alright, Robin." The way he says it reminds me of when we were children, only then it was the opposite.

He'd never admit back then that there was hope. Never.

"Let me show you your room," he says and then he blows out a low steady whistle. My muscles tighten as the large German shepherd trots into the room. With his tongue hanging out just slightly and his ears sticking straight up, he looks approachable, friendly even. But I can't breathe.

"Jay," I say his name like a warning.

Jay bends down, crouching on the floor and petting the dog's head with both of his hands. "We have to face our fears, don't we?" he says with a sad smile. I remember the scar on his leg from when he was a boy, and I take a hesitant step forward.

"Is that why you got him?" I ask him, but keep my eyes on the dog. My palms itch with a faint sweat, and my heart races. It took me years to overcome my fear of them. Even my family dog when I got home, a golden retriever named Chloe who was almost eight years old scared the shit out of me when she barked. I cried constantly, unable to stop the fear and the pounding of my heart, but knowing it wouldn't go away. It wasn't her fault. I loved her before, but the barking only reminded me of the terror I'd run away from.

Jay follows the dog, leaving me watching and forcing my legs to move forward.

The hall is small and short, and all of the doors are closed, but they have character. The house is old. Although the fixtures are new and the paint fresh, it's designed like an older home. The doors are carved and made of hard maple. My fingertips glide along the wall and then dip to a door and back up to the plaster wall.

"Whose house is this?" I ask Jay to change the subject.

"Mine," he answers without turning around and steps into a door at the very end. A door that's closest to the end of the hallway and the opening to the living room. I grip the inside of the doorway, partly to keep me from running, but also to make sure Jay knows I'm not leaving as I lean out and take a look.

The ceiling is tall, taller than I imagined for the

hallway being so small. A large ceiling fan whirls and the small gust makes the floor to ceiling curtains sway. They're thin fabric with an organic quality to them.

Lots of browns. Dark brown floors, the tab top curtains and dark wood furniture are everywhere. The only hint of color is the dark blue sofa and matching love seat that sit in front of the large windows. With the curtains being so thin, I can see all the surroundings. Even through the gray of the sky and the slightly blurred view from the rain, it's picturesque, with the field of green and mountains way back in the distance.

But it sends a chill through me. I decided I'll stay, but I never really had a choice. The realization is sobering.

I focus on the furniture, on the living room itself. It's almost like a cabin, but modernized with a comfortable feel to it. It's homey, but barren in every other sense. There's no artwork. Nothing hanging on the walls. There are no candles or knickknacks. No books or magazines. No throw pillows or blankets. There isn't even a TV.

"Do you live here then?" I ask him, leaning back and looking over my shoulder to Jay. I still haven't stopped gripping the doorjamb.

He looks at me hard for a moment, as if debating on telling me and finally he nods once. "It's beautiful," I say just above a murmur.

I look down the hallway again and gesture with a nod. "Which is your room?" I ask him.

His voice is empty of every emotion when he answers, "The basement." My heart squeezes in my chest, and I have to tear my eyes away from him. All this time, I've been moving forward, trying to have a normal life. And Jay's merely been holding on to the past.

I have to close my eyes as the German shepherd rubs against my leg, the feel of his wiry fur sending chills through my stiffened body as he pants and leaves the room, laying with a loud thud in the hallway.

"He frightens you?" Jay asks me, and I whip my head to him.

"He bit me." I grit my teeth after saying the words because it's not quite true.

Jay takes three large strides toward me, closing the space between us and placing his hand over mine, still clinging to the doorway.

"Toby," Jay says with his eyes locked on mine although he's calling for the dog. He whistles low as the large dog rises and trots obediently to wait by his master.

I only resist slightly as Jay pulls my hand down, crouching and making me bend at the waist. I close my eyes, but continue to breathe evenly.

He won't hurt me. Not Toby or Jay. He won't hurt me. I repeat this over and over in my head, focusing on breathing.

The dog's tongue laps at my hand, feeling like rough sandpaper and I slowly open my eyes.

"He likes you," Jay says without looking at me, petting the dog and releasing my hand. "I knew he would," he says and pats the dog's head before standing up. The moment he does, Toby stops licking me and sits, waiting for another order.

"He won't let you leave," Jay says as he shoves both of his hands into his jeans pockets and stares down the hall at the door to the basement. He takes in a heavy breath and looks at me. "He's a good boy, but he won't let you leave."

I nod my head once, searching Jay's eyes for sympathy or guilt, but there's nothing there. The dog pants for a moment, and Jay waves him off with his hand.

"You didn't seem to mind the dogs before," Jay says as he turns his back, leaving me in the hall to watch as Toby stretches along the dark hardwood floor in the opening to the living room. The fan is on, and the faint breeze ruffles his fur.

It's only when I turn, pulling my eyes away from the dog that I register Jay's words. "What dogs?" I ask him as my heart beats harder.

I take a look at him as he walks into a nearby room. He picks up something small off the dresser, and I recognize it instantly. I'm stunned as I take a step into the room and realize it's not just any room.

This is *my* room.

"IF YOU COULD BE ANYWHERE YOU'D LIKE, WHERE WOULD IT *be?" he asks me.*

I shift on the floor, my shoulder feeling numb. I pick at my broken nails and look at the floor where I've been picking at the ground. There's never anything to do. Nothing but talk to Jay.

I can't stand it when he's gone. It's the fear of not knowing if he'll come back. The fear of not knowing what I'll become if his father takes him away from me forever.

"Hey," I hear Jay say softly, "just talk to me."

I stare at him, bewildered. He's different today. Softer in a lot of ways. "If you could go anywhere at all, where would it be?"

I pull my legs into my chest, feeling my back stretch as I close my eyes. "In a castle in Ireland," I say jokingly with a smile. Deep down my heart hurts because I know what I really think. Back home with my family. But I'm not allowed to talk about that. Jay doesn't like it when I bring them up.

"Ireland?" he asks with curiosity. I shrug my shoulders and let out a small sigh.

"There's a picture from one of my books at home. It's a room in a castle." I feel my cheeks heat with embarrassment as I remember it's from a fairytale. I won't tell him that. I'm already younger than Jay. I don't want him to think of me like I'm a little kid although that's exactly how he sees me.

"I thought you'd say Disneyland," he says and laughs at me, rolling onto his back and passing the ball back and forth between his hands. It's odd to see anything at all in the room. The ball moves from palm to palm rhythmically and I see a smile grow on the boy's face. He looks so young, smiling as he lies on the ground, fiddling with a baseball.

It was a present, he told me, a present for being good.

I sit up on the floor, my palm brushing against the concrete that's all too familiar. "Do you think he'll let us go outside and play with it?" I ask him.

He stops his wrist in mid-motion, gripping the ball tightly in his right hand and almost dropping it.

"There is no outside, little bird," he says and then looks up at me, a small smile trying to curl his lips up, but it's so sad. I swallow the lump in my throat as he adds, "But we can pretend to be anywhere."

Although my heart breaks and tears fill my eyes, Jay sits up *and hands me the ball, forcing it into my hand and sitting cross-legged across from me.*

"Tell me about your room, Robin. I want to know all about it."

***

MY EYES GLIDE ACROSS THE ROOM, TAKING IN EVERY INCH of it. Again, the ceilings are so high up. Higher than I realized at first, and the cream ceiling is fitted with dark wood beams that make my eyes travel up. A thin white chandelier with small crystals and lights that look like candles brightens the room. There are two smaller ones on either side of the bed which sits on the far end of the room along the wall. The headboard is the same dark wood as the beams, and it travels up the height of the wall.

It's hard edges and darkness are at complete odds with the bed itself, which is plush and littered with small cream pillows decorated with crystals and embroidery that my fingers long to touch.

"I made it for you," Jay says softly and I turn to him, not knowing what to say.

"Everything you need is here. I brought what you needed from your old place, too."

Your old place. The words make a chill travel down my spine, but I ignore it, letting my body move through the room, opening the drawers to the armoire and seeing my own things alongside others Jay's bought for me.

"I had to take your phone though and your computer, for obvious reasons."

"People will start to question-" I start to tell him, but he cuts me off.

"I've taken care of it." He sets down the object he's been playing with in his hands and its only then that I see what it is. It's a wooden owl, a trinket I got from my mom back in college. I watch him place it back on the dresser, exactly where it sat on my dresser at home. "If they text you, they'll get a message about you being on vacation and in an area with little reception. An email will get them the same thing."

"Take a look around, Robin. This is your new home, at least for a little while." My blood chills as he adds, "Your sabbatical is for eight weeks." I start to think about everyone who might call. My parents, maybe. My mom calls once a month. Other than her, possibly Karen. But this wouldn't be the first time I ghosted. They won't stop trying though. They'll come for me. The thought makes me tear my eyes away from Jay. I grip the bedpost as I try to calm myself.

I'm staying. I've already decided, and this changes nothing. I swallow the fears and take in the rest of the room, very aware of how Jay's eyes follow me.

My feet sink into the woven cream carpet as I walk toward the far wall.

There are curved shutters on the wall painted in a pale blue. Two sets of them that are shut and line up perfectly to form the shape of a leaf, the tips meeting in the very center.

They're exactly what I described to Jay so long ago.

Like the shutters in the castle of my fairytale. My feet move of their own accord and I slide my fingers over the slats of painted wood and slowly open them. But behind them is nothing.

Not the mountains and green fields that I could see in the living room. Just the flat wall.

My fingers tremble as I close the shutters and slowly turn to Jay.

This is my room, and it's a prison of my own making.

CHAPTER 13

Jay

My eyes follow her as she moves, almost like she did the first night I saw her. She looked around the barren basement back then with different expectations.

My little bird likes her gilded cage, but she's not a fool. She knows that's exactly what it is. Seeing her here in my clothes, in the room I made just for her... it makes me want more.

I swallow as my blood heats and I watch her close the shutters.

"The bathroom is through here," I tell her, and she turns quickly to face me. I hate myself for bricking over the windows. She loved looking outside, but that was all she did, pined for freedom and somewhere else to go. I can't have that here. I can't give her any bit of it. I won't tempt her to leave me. She's already proven that I can't trust her. She ran the first chance she got. *I knew she would.*

She walks carefully toward me as I gesture to the door across the hallway. I let her pass me, following my instruction and getting a faint hint of her scent. That sweet floral is still there, but she needs to be bathed.

My dick hardens as I walk behind her, watching as she grips the oil rubbed bronze doorknob to the bathroom but then looks back at me for permission. My head nods on its own, somehow able to function even though internally I'm tortured by what I'm doing to her.

The light brightens the room and reflects off of the white marble tile. Everything is white and sterile in the bathroom, except for the black penny tile arranged in an ordered fashion on the floor. Even the curtain to the claw foot tub is a simple white.

She lets her fingers glide along the granite counter to the sink and I take a step through the door to get in with her. My blood heats as I close the space between us and she turns around to face me, surprised.

I'll give her what she needs, and she'll give me what I need.

"You need a bath," I tell her simply as I shut the door behind me. Her eyes flick to the doorknob and then back to me as she takes a step behind her.

"Jay?" she asks. She's always said my name like that. Like she's asking for permission, for comfort, for anything and everything when she breathes my name. Because what I say is true to her. There is only what my answer is and she will believe it with everything she has. There's so much power in how she expresses it. So much weakness in her voice.

"Yes?" I ask her, feigning nonchalance as I lean against

the sink. I cross my arms and wait for her to say what's on her mind. I wait for her to address the fact that I desperately want to fuck her.

She can barely breathe as she stands in front of me.

"I've seen you plenty of times, Robin," I finally admit to her. I watch her eyes as I tell her, "I've come to your house a few times." I wait for her reaction. I expect fear or disgust, or maybe some mix of both. But she merely nods and slowly pushes the pants down her legs.

The bathroom is small and the sound of the pajama pants bunching and pooling around her legs and then at her feet fills the room. It's all I can hear along with the thumping of my heart. She's hesitant to take off the shirt though. Her fingers play along the hem and she looks back at me with nothing but insecurities.

"I'm not going to hurt you, Robin." I hate that she would ever think that. Her eyes remain skeptical, and she doesn't make a move to take it off. "There was only one time I ever wanted to hurt you."

That gets a reaction from her, but it's not one I want. It takes me a moment before I even realize how she's taken it.

I clear my throat and grit my teeth as my hand goes to the back of my head and I try to explain. "I was there that night when you took the bottle of pills and swallowed them."

"I've never been so angry, Robin." My breathing picks up as I remember. By the time I ran around to the front of her house and broke in, she was already throwing up in the bathroom.

"You saw?" she asks softly. She covers her face and

turns away from me. She shakes her head softly and the need to comfort and hold her takes over, but as soon as I approach, she turns around and takes a step backward.

I tell her as I take a step forward, "I'm not angry with you anymore." Her shoulders rise and fall as she waits for my next move.

She's my prey, small and scared. And trapped.

But I think she likes it this way. I think I'm her predator of choice.

"You were alone, and you carry so much guilt with you that isn't fair."

I wrap my hand around her waist as her legs hit the toilet and her hand brushes against the closed curtain to the tub. My blunt fingernails dig in as I pull her close to me. At first her hands come up, ready to brace her palms against my chest. But she knows better, and she quickly grabs on to the bit of her shirt on her upper thighs.

I let her chest hit me and hold her gaze as she stares into my eyes. "Robin," I lick my lips and then tell her, "I've wanted so much from you for so long."

I close my eyes as the years pass before me. My concern growing into an obsession. I open them to find her hazel eyes swirled with desire. Her breathing in short pants.

I lower my lips to her neck and whisper, "I don't want to wait any longer."

Robin reaches up just as the words slip past my lips. My initial instinct is to grab her, to force her back and pin her down. To protect myself. But her fingers spear through my hair and she crashes her lips against mine before I can admonish her. Her eyes are closed as she kisses me with longing, sweet and slow, but also a desperation that matches my own. I splay my hand along her back and trail my fingers up her thigh and over the dip of her waist. Her lips soften as I move my hand to her neck, my thumb brushing along her jaw.

I've dreamed of this moment for so long.

Her breath is hot and mingles with my own as I feel her soft skin, letting my hands roam freely and relaxing my grip on her. Her touch is soft, as I knew it would be. She's gentle but needy. Greedy, even. I pull back slightly and she lets me, but she's slow to open her eyes. She doesn't want it to stop. The thought makes my dick twitch and I grip her hips and move her ass to sit on the counter. Like the good girl she is, she parts her legs for me and I nestle my hips between her thighs.

"I want you, Jay," she whispers the words like a confession. Her eyes are still closed, and I can see how much it pains her to admit it. It's because I'm broken. She thinks this is wrong when it's the only thing that feels right.

I brush the tip of my nose along hers, waiting for her to look at me. She's out of breath and her eyes are a mix of emotions. She needs me as much as I need her.

I cup her chin in my hand and brush my thumb along her lower lip. "I would give anything to have all of you," I admit to her with absolute truth.

"Will you let me touch you?" she asks me, and my heart stops.

It's only my chest where I don't like being touched. I can still feel my father's hands slamming against me over and over. Pushing me backward. I don't fight it. I let him because if I don't, it's so much worse.

My blood rushes in my ears as I nod my head once. I should've guessed it was coming. I suppose in a lot of ways it was, because I'm ready for it. I want her to do what she wants to me. And I to her.

"I know I need this," I tell her. I'm so fucking aware of how damaged I am. "I don't want to be like this," I whisper and then pull the shirt over my head. The thin cotton slides up my back and over my shoulders until I'm facing her with nothing to hide me. Her eyes focus on my chest and dance along the faint scars.

They aren't horrible to look at, mostly faded from the two decades of time between now and then.

I can hear her breathe as she moves closer to me. She peeks up at me and I can almost hear my name on her lips. Asking me for permission, but I nod before she can do it. "Go ahead," I tell her with my shoulders squared. I may be broken, but I want to be fixed. I want her touch in every way.

Her hand shakes just over my chest. So close I can already feel the heat from her. I brace myself for it. For her touch. I want it more than anything. I want to feel her fingertips run along my scars and not cause me pain and shame.

If ever someone could do it, it would be her. I halt my breathing as she rests her middle finger along the dip in my throat and then slowly lowers it, trailing down the faint silver of a small scar. It's not the worst of them.

I wish I knew what they were from. I wish I still had the memories of what it was that left each of them. But there were so many, and time confuses things. The one on my leg was from the dog. The largest of the three. The one who almost killed me. That's the only scar I can place in my past. The rest are merely a summary of what my father gave me.

I grip her wrist out of instinct when she moves lower. She stays still, waiting for me. "I think that's enough for now, little bird," I say with my eyes closed and then look down at her.

"Jay, I promise I'll stay." Her voice is pleading but also sincere. I don't like her tone though. I gave her what she wanted, so she needs to give me what I want in return. "I promise I'll stay with you and beside you, and that I want what you want. I promise you," she pleads with me, and I already know what she's going to say.

"Just come with me to get help."

I stare into her hazel eyes as they gloss over with unshed tears.

Help. She is my help. She is the reason I'm like this. My breathing gets heavy as I resist the urge to snap.

Leave? No. We're only getting started.

She left me once, and she'll do it again. There's a sorcery about her, something that distracts me from the reality. Something that makes me feel as though just caring for her will be enough to heal all wounds. I bend down, picking up my shirt and put it on quickly, covering the scars from her view.

"Get a bath," I tell her and turn my back to her, opening the bathroom door and feeling the gush of cold air flood the room. "Don't make me regret leaving you alone."

CHAPTER 14

Robin

*I*t's so quiet. Every small movement is accompanied by the sounds of the blanket shifting. There's not the faintest noise except the ones I create.

A little while ago the air conditioner kicked on, and it was heaven. A bit of white noise to drown out the silence. But the break was short-lived, so instead, I lie here in silence.

I turn over onto my side and pick at the threads on the comforter. They're small and so easily pulled.

I close my eyes and the vision of the basement flashes before my eyes. It was quiet then, too. But at least I had the steady sounds of Jay behind me. My throat feels tight as I swallow and try to calm myself down.

I think of the city noise and focus on it. So many nights it's kept me from this very nightmare. It's not so loud that it keeps me up or disturbs my sleep. But it's loud enough to keep me from going back *there* in my mind.

I grit my teeth and think of how he could hold me now. If he wanted to, he could be in here. I could sleep again.

The thought of falling into the depths of a dream with him makes my body move on its own. I throw back the heavy comforter and move from the bed with purposeful strides but hesitate at the door, my heart beating harder and my confidence waning by the second.

I swallow thickly, my heart beating slowly as fear creeps up and nearly stops me. But how many nights have I prayed to be close to him? How many nights have I wanted him to hold me? And he's so close. I only have to ask.

My heart aches in my chest as I remember how he'd whisper it. *If you need me, just ask.*

I need him. God, do I need him.

The lump seems to stop in my throat mid-swallow as I grip the doorknob and open it slowly. It doesn't escape me that there's no lock. Just like the bathroom. None to force me to stay in the room, and none to keep Jay out.

The door's silent, which is a blessing and a curse.

I don't want Jay to think I'm leaving.

Or worse, the dog.

I peek my head out of the doorway, opening it up slowly to reveal more of the hall. The moonlight spills into the front of the hall from the window in the living room and floods it with light. So much more than what I have in the room Jay gave to me.

I only take one step, my bare foot making the floor groan with my weight before I hear a low growl.

"Toby," I hear Jay's voice say the dog's name low and with an admonition in his voice just as the fear was about to take me. "Stay," Jay orders from the living room. I turn my head to look back down the hall to the closed door to the basement. That's where I was headed, but I follow the sound of Jay's voice and walk slowly to the living room, gripping the molding that cases the doorway and facing both Jay and Toby.

Jay's on his back in the middle of the floor. A thin blanket covers his lower body, and Toby lays close to Jay. He doesn't turn to look at me. He absentmindedly pets the dog once and then twice while staring at the ceiling. If not from his hand stroking the dog, I'd think he was asleep with his eyes open, his body is so still.

The dog merely lifts his head once, assessing me and then laying his head back down as if he's content with my presence.

"I wasn't sneaking out," I say quickly and the way I said it makes even me think that I was lying. My fingers twist around one another as I chance a step closer to Jay, just one, although my eyes stay on the dog.

"You should be sleeping, little bird," Jay finally says and then turns his head to look at me.

"I wanted," I start to say but get caught in his gaze. It's intense and the way his eyes look at night with him being so tired, takes me back to when we were trapped. Back to when he couldn't sleep at all.

"Will you lie down with me?" I manage to ask him, although I don't know how.

"No," he answers quickly and with finality. My heart feels splintered from his cold denial. I nod once, accepting it and trying not to think back to the bathroom. To the kiss. To the moment I thought we had. The moment I ruined.

It's my fault. It's all my fault.

"Leave the door open," Jay says softly, ignoring how I'm barely holding on.

I nod my head again and bite my lip as I turn my back to him, to go back alone to the room. It's only then that Jay says, "I can't, Robin. John will be here soon."

John. The way Jay talks about him makes my heart ache with a splintering pain that's nearly debilitating. I have to wait a moment, forcing all of the emotions away. Taking a look at this from my clinical background.

"What's the purpose of doing things this way?" I lick my lips after croaking out the words. I'm nervous to approach Jay; after all the years of training, I should be more confident. But it's Jay. I'm afraid to touch him, or to hurt him, to make him angry. Not because of what he'd do to me, but because of what my words could do to him.

Words are powerful, so much more than we realize.

"What do you mean?" he asks me, still staring at the ceiling, but his relaxed body is now stiff and his response makes me shift uneasily. I decide to sit on the ground, still in the entrance. The thin nightgown rides up but I pull it down as the cold wood floor presses against my thighs.

"Your way," I answer him and put my hands in my lap. It feels like a session in some ways, and the thought is comforting. "Why do you want to do it like this?" I ask him.

"John won't listen to me," Jay says. "He just shuts me down and he doesn't hear it."

"You talk to him often?" I ask him as I pick at the hem of my nightgown, each little bit of information helps me to understand.

Jay clears his throat roughly and looks away from me and toward the window. My throat closes, hating how much this wounds him.

"That's fine," I tell him to try to reassure him. "I understand, Jay." I keep my voice light and calm, feigning a casual air about such a serious conversation. "You know I'd never judge you." I try to speak the words calmly, but they're quiet at the end as the anguish rises and my throat seems to close. My shoulders rise slowly as I take in a deep steadying breath and close my eyes.

"He won't be able to deny you," Jay says and his words make my eyes open. He licks his lips as soon as my eyes reach his, and they draw my focus to his mouth.

My body heats, and I feel nothing but ashamed. The desire is there; I can't help it. But I'm ashamed that in this moment I want to comfort him in a primitive way. I have to tear my eyes away as I ask, "So you need me to tell him about our past? You can see why that scares me, can't you?"

He shakes his head and says, "You don't have to tell him anything you don't want to." My eyes flick back to his as he swallows and adds, "I just thought hearing it from you would help."

"Since he won't listen to you," I say as if it's a question, but it's only to clarify what I already know. I try my best to hide the genuine fear of revealing anything to John. But I fail at it, miserably.

A hesitant breath leaves me and I try to beg him one last time, "We should go-"

He cuts me off before I can finish and says, "I'll protect you. Always. I'll be there."

Always. The word is the final dagger. "You can't promise me that." I lower my head as the words slip out and I lose my sense of composure. I rest my head in my hands, my fingers spearing through my hair and I rock forward slightly. I'm not normally like this. The last time was my final session with Marie.

She reminded me so much of Jay. So much of me. So much of what we'd been through.

But this is nothing like what that poor girl went through. There's only so much a person can be pushed. Only so much pain they can handle before they break. She wouldn't take the medication I prescribed, and she couldn't turn off the nightmares.

I can't break down again. I can't let what happened to Marie happen to Jay. I have to be strong for those who can't. I failed her.

"I can, and I will. Please, little bird, my Robin." Jay rises and crawls to me. I peek up through my lashes, wet with the promise of tears that I hold back.

I don't resist him when he wraps his arms around me and pulls me into his lap. I stay still, not reaching up like I did when I was a child. He'd hold me if I promised not to hold him back.

But his grip on me is so different now. Everything is different.

The way the warmth of his strong body envelops me and heats my blood.

The way our breath mingles and begs me to arch my neck and press my lips against his.

The way I lean into his chest and breathe in his scent. He's slow to react when I place my hand on his thigh. He shushes me, cautiously, as if he's not sure that's what he wants to do. Slowly, he bends forward and kisses my neck.

This is so horribly wrong.

I need to be stronger than this. Stronger for Jay.

"How does this end?" I ask him.

He gives me a sad smile. "I don't know, little bird," he says looking down at me. "I don't know what will happen when he finds out."

I start to answer him, but the moment my lips open with a quick breath, he cuts me off.

"You need to go to bed."

"Can I sleep with you?" I ask him although I hate myself for it. I crave his comfort, and I know he craves mine. He gently pushes a strand of hair from my face and tucks it behind my ear, looking at me all the while with a tortured gaze.

"I want to touch you," Jay says and the sadness in his voice is outweighed by desire.

"Then touch me," I whisper, but it only cues him to stand, leaving me on the floor and staring up at him, the hope dimming with each passing second.

"I don't trust myself," he finally says and I shake my head, wiping the sleep and misery from my eyes.

The shame overwhelms me again. I'm so fucked up

and broken for wanting him, but I do, so badly. Jay's hand grips my chin, forcing me to look up at him although the touch is comforting.

"It's not you, Robin," he tells me and before I can answer him with a sarcastic remark he says, "I want to make it hurt." His eyes are dark as he lets his hand fall. He turns his back to me as I let his words sink in. The muscles in his broad shoulders ripple in the dim light as he walks away from me, leaving me behind and he says with finality, "Now go to bed."

CHAPTER 15

Robin

I roll over with a groan. The click of a door opening and closing wakes me from my sleep. My eyes hurt, and my head feels heavy. I didn't sleep enough, but the second I come to, I don't want to sleep.

Jay. I make a move to get off the bed, but my leg hits something hot and heavy.

I almost scream at the sight of Toby on the sheets, his jaws opening wide with a yawn. It's a lazy yawn, as if there's not a damn thing wrong in this dog's life. He stretches on the bed as I slowly creep away, my heart beating fast even though I repeat to myself over and over that it's okay. Not all dogs are the same. Just like people.

"He doesn't want to hurt me," I whisper with my eyes closed and when I open them, he's staring back at me.

I notice the flecks of yellow in his chocolate brown eyes. His tongue laps along his sharp teeth and it's all I can focus on for a moment, but only a moment before the big beast whines at me. The cry is strange as he whimpers and lowers his head, as if I've hurt him.

It takes me a moment, his big eyes on me before I climb off the bed, on the far side of the room. My toes hit the plush carpet and the absence of the warmth of the covers leaves goosebumps down my arms and legs. The silk nightgown is simply too thin for the early morning.

The dog's head raises and he springs from the bed, his large paws thudding on the floor as he rounds the bed. He watches me for a moment before pacing to the door. He's anxious as he looks back at me.

I worry that he won't let me shut the door, that he'll stay there in the doorway, both keeping me in here and also being too close for comfort. I've tried so long to rid myself of the fear of dogs and for a long time, it was bearable. But right now, it's just too much.

"I'm sorry," I tell Toby as he looks back at me with those eyes, like he doesn't know what to do with me or what to think of me.

"It's not you," I try to talk to the dog, feeling guilty because of the look in his eyes, but the sound of steady steps approaching stops me mid-thought. My heart sputters and turns in my chest as Toby moves out of the room and to the right toward the living room.

"Robin?" I hear his voice before I see him, and already I know it's John.

He stops in the doorway, his broad frame filling it, with nothing but denim jeans and a crisp white undershirt on although there's a black smear, obviously a stain on the lower left side. His boots are already on and I find myself staring at them, my heart aching and my throat going dry.

"Are you alright?" he asks me with a lowered voice, looking down the hallway before placing his hand on the middle of the door and pushing it open a bit more. He looks worried, concerned for me and like he's going to take me away. Like he thinks I want to sneak out.

There's more stubble lining his jaw today than there was yesterday, and his eyes are red. He didn't sleep.

"I didn't sleep well," I admit to him and avert my eyes as I pick at the hem of my thin nightgown. I wonder what John thinks of me. Of this. Of yesterday, or at least what he knows of it.

John runs his hand through his hair and looks back down the hall again. I can see the words on his lips, the promise to help. Asking me if I want to leave.

But I could never do that.

"When will you be back?" I ask him casually and tuck a strand of hair behind my ear. I take a step closer to him and cross my arms over my chest.

"I won't be long," he says with uncertainty.

"I'll be here when you get back," I tell him confidently and feign a smile. I'm sure it doesn't reach my eyes, but I don't care. It does what it's meant to. It gets him to leave without an attempt to take me away.

"I'm looking forward to our session," I say and keep my voice hopeful as I keep his gaze.

A confused look mars John's face as he leaves, Toby turning his massive head to follow him.

"I'll be back soon," he says looking over his shoulder

and patting his hand on the doorway once, hesitating to take a step, but leaving me alone.

I nervously pick at my fingernails, remembering the camera, knowing that I have to go backward in time, back to what haunts me at night, back to what John doesn't know.

CHAPTER 16

John

I don't even remember work today. My hands moved on their own, the task at hand blurring with what was consuming my mind.

The thought of her in the house. *Left with Jay.*

I finished one order. The only one I had that would bring anyone to my shop at all.

For now, and for the time being, the shop is closed. And every waking moment will be spent in that house with Robin.

I'm not leaving her again.

The doorknob clicks as I sneak into 401 Cadence Square, slipping the pin I used to unlock it into my back jeans pocket. My blood rushes through my veins. I know this is illegal, technically breaking and entering and I look over my shoulder before closing the door behind me. I swallow hard and let out an uneasy breath as I look around the living room.

Residence to Miss Robin Everly. Or former residence, unbeknownst to the rest of the world.

I walk easily into the cozy space. It's a small ranch house that's fairly dated, but her furniture and décor are modern and mostly simple. It's the pop of colors and textures that give it life. They seem odd knowing the bit of her she's shown me.

There's a professionalism about the room. Organization that seems more fit for a home design magazine, but the colors are cheery. Bright teal in the designs of the throw pillows and pale yellow stripes on the curtains and rugs. There are a scattering of teal flowers and motivational sayings like 'Live, Laugh, Love' on the pictures throughout the place.

As if she needs to be surrounded by something to keep out the stark and cold emptiness that would be left if those pieces were removed.

I ignore them for a moment, feeling my stomach churn at the thought of her being here instead of in the cabin. My phone is heavy in my hand as I watch the screen for a moment.

I have six cameras – not like the one Jay has set up in the basement. This way I can watch everything, at all times. He doesn't know a thing about them, and he doesn't need to. This is my insurance. I stare at the screen, watching how she sits across from the dog. She's cross-legged and the dog's laying down, but eyeing her curiously.

I wonder if Jay told her Toby is for emotional support. My fingers itched to touch her hand, to hold it while I let Toby approach her. Jay was right when he said she was damaged. He was right when he said she needed help.

I could help her. And I will. With or without Jay. If I'm going to do this, I'm going to do this right.

The only reason I'm not there now is that I need to know more about her. And see if I can find the evidence Jay left behind. The anger rises slowly. It's always like that when I think of Jay. A slow rise that turns to a simmer. Usually the thought that he can't help it is enough to calm me, but he fucking set me up. He forced my hand, and that's something that's unforgivable.

I slip the phone into my back pocket, turning my head to the window on the left side of the room as the gentle city traffic is disrupted with a honking horn.

I'm quiet as I walk through the house, greeted only by silence. My instinct is to go to her bedroom, but when the door creaks open and I peek in, I see her bed first. The sheets and comforter are in disarray and there's broken glass on the floor.

Fuck! Jay told me he left evidence, but I didn't expect it to be something so fucking obvious.

I grit my teeth and go back to the tiny galley kitchen, reaching into my other back pocket for the thin black leather gloves. I'm careful with every step.

The cabinets are old and worn. I have to go through three of them before I find the dust pan. I take my time, cleaning up the room and wiping down every surface I can think of. All the while I take in every inch of her place.

What's most odd is that it feels like I've already been here. Especially the bedroom. It feels like I know her, like we aren't strangers in the least. I can't shake the feeling; I haven't been able to since I first laid eyes on that photograph.

I toss the rag I've been using to wipe down surfaces into the trash bag in her kitchen as the unsettling thought passes through me.

I make a mental note to take the trash with me on the way out. No piece of evidence left behind. I don't know when she'll be back...

I was going to let her go this morning. I was ready to take her with me. I'd do what I have to do with Jay and plead with her to stay with me until I figured a way out, but she was so willing to remain when I left. So unlike what I anticipated.

It feels like a trap.

I let the unfinished thought slip away as I think I hear someone in the living room.

My eyes whip up to the small doorway and I wait, listening to the blood rushing in my ears. *Thump, thump, thump, thump.* My heart races in my chest.

I'm quick to remove the gloves, shoving them in my back pocket and waiting for whoever it is to say or do something. I anticipate them calling out her name to see if she's home. But there's nothing but silence until Jay appears in the doorway.

A smirk slowly lifts his lips up with a knowing glint that sparkles in his eyes.

"Fucking bastard," I mutter under my breath. The smile widens and he walks closer to me.

"Cleaning up?" he asks me and then glances at the trash bag.

"Yeah," I answer him and bend down to tie it off. "Just on my way out," I tell him.

"You should go," Jay says, his voice full of something I've never heard from him before. Possessiveness, jealousy even. He leans his back against the doorway, blocking part of the exit and adds, "She's waiting for you."

There's an undertone to his voice that accompanies his narrowed eyes as he cracks his knuckles one by one. "You'll have to tell me what you think of your session."

I crack my own knuckles, mirroring him. "What I think about her, you mean?" I ask him, pushing him just slightly to see what his intentions are, to pick at the real meaning behind his question.

A rough laugh escapes his lips as he tilts his head and looks me in the eyes, crossing his arms as he shrugs. "I already know what you think of her," he says in a low voice, almost a murmur. Like it wasn't meant for me, which pisses me off.

"Is that right?" I ask him, feeling my blood heat and adrenaline coursing through me. It's been a long time since we've gotten into it. But I can feel it coming. Maybe not today while she's trapped at the cabin. But when she's safe, I know it's going to happen.

He relaxes his posture, as if coming to the same conclusion at the very same time. It does an odd thing to me and I want to bite the question back, but I can't anymore.

"Do you love her?" I ask him.

The smile stays on his face as he answers immediately, "Of course I do. If I didn't, I never would have let her go."

Jay admits to what I already knew. The love between

them is obvious. The thing that shocks me is how hearing the words on his lips makes me feel. *Jealous.*

"Then let her go again. Let her make that choice," I tell him words I know are rational, even if what I'm feeling is anything but.

"We're only just getting started," Jay says as he turns to leave.

"You told me it was about her," I yell at him as he's leaving, letting my emotions get the best of me. My words halt his footsteps. He turns to look over his shoulders, his eyes smoldering with an intensity I've never seen.

"It's all about her. It's always been about her."

"I find that really fucking hard to believe right now," I spit as I take a step forward, meeting him halfway.

"Don't forget who will take the fall for this if something happens, John," Jay sneers my name, his eyes darkening with anger.

His threat means nothing to me; I don't care what the consequences are anymore. He smiles at me, a wicked grin at the thought. "She's just as much for you as she is me," he says and I flinch. "She has something she hasn't told you, John. Something you *need* to hear."

My body freezes as I watch him step back into the small kitchen. He carelessly touches every cabinet.

"What is it?" I ask him, not sure if I believe him or if this is a mind game to get me to do what he wants. But something feels off with her. A familiarity I can't grasp. A pull so strong that it makes me reckless.

He stops and looks back at me, a flash of fear in his expression, but only for a moment. "I want her to tell you," he says quietly.

I shake my head; there's nothing she could tell me that would change anything. But as I look up to tell Jay just that, he stares back at me with an expression I can't place. He drops his eyes and stares at the linoleum kitchen floor as a moment passes, letting the anger dim.

"I just need a little more time. Just a little longer before it all changes." He says the words so quietly, like they aren't for me. Only for himself.

"Before what changes?" I ask him as he turns to leave. He looks up at me like he forgot I was even here.

He stares at me for a moment, debating on answering me before saying, "Everything."

CHAPTER 17

Robin

The red light makes me angrier today than it did the first time.

A conditioned environment makes sense. If you want someone to remember something, you recreate it. You offer up any triggers, any objects or words that could have a mental association. Jay's plan has merit.

But it makes me angry because it takes me back there. Back to when I was helpless. Back to when I didn't fight. If I had known how it would end, I would have killed the bastard. I would have found a way. I would have killed him before he could hurt Jay anymore.

My shoulders are squared as I sit on the bed though. My back's against the hard cinder block wall. It doesn't slip by me that John's back is to the drywall, and he's the one who's forced to stare at the block wall. The same fucking stone that tortured my vision for four straight months.

"Do you feel comfortable?" John asks as he leans forward and puts his hands between his knees. I try to keep my eyes from moving to the blinking red light, but I fail.

I swallow the lump in my throat. "I could be more comfortable," I tell him and then look back to his steely gaze, "but I'll be fine."

"You seem…" his brow furrows and he leans back with an uncomfortable expression. "Better today," he concludes, finally settling on the words he wants.

"I'm more certain of what I need to do," I look into the swirls of gray clouds as I tell him and bring my knees up to my chest. It's an odd behavior I've seen patients do, but I like it when they do it. It makes them vulnerable, which inherently means they're not defensive.

My eyes drift back to the red light, and I wonder who's really running this session. It needs to be me.

"Can I tell you something?" I ask John although it's a rhetorical question.

He nods his head once, not breaking my gaze and says, "Jay said you had something to tell me." My blood turns cold and I swallow the unforgiving lump in my throat, lowering my head to the comforter. I pull it up tighter around me, not wanting to address what John's said at all. So, I don't.

I pick at a loose thread. It's a habit because for so long, all I had was a blanket to pick at. This one is thicker, higher quality and clean, but it's a blanket nonetheless.

The thin thread slips between my fleshy fingertips before sliding past my nails as I start my story. "This story is about a girl named Marie." Just saying her name makes my heart squeeze in my chest.

Her face flashes before my eyes. Beautiful green eyes that were so clear and so pure, I felt she could see to the very depths of my soul. Her skin was pale and her hair was always combed just so. She kept it perfectly straight as though she were put together, but she wasn't in the least.

"Marie?" John asks me, and then crosses his ankle over his knee. The movement makes me look up as the memory of her voice echoes in my ears. *Doctor Everly.*

I nod my head, hating how real her voice sounds.

It takes me a moment before I'm able to speak. "She had a very abusive father. Her mother fled in the middle of the night when she was only six and left her there."

The pain is nearly consuming as I talk about her in the past tense, but that's where Marie will always be. Never again to be here with me.

"He hurt her?" John asks, and it disrupts my thoughts. I part my lips to exhale and answer his question. "Badly."

"I'm sorry to hear that," John says with true sympathy. "You knew her well?"

My hair brushes my cheeks as I nod and say, "I was her shrink."

"For almost ten years he systematically abused her in every way possible."

"That's horrible," John says although his voice is absent. I feel the need to look up, to look into his eyes to see what he's thinking, but I can't. All I can picture is how Marie looked the last time I saw her. I knew she wasn't well, but they wouldn't let me go to her. They wouldn't let me keep her from leaving. She left me, and I knew it was the last time I'd see her.

"I couldn't save her," I whisper and let the warm tears slide down my cheeks. "I begged her, the last time I saw her, I begged her to take her medication but she didn't believe it would work."

Marie never had a chance. The moment she was saved from her father, the true beast destroyed her. Her memory.

The home she was in was temporary, and they didn't care for her. They just wanted a check. The city bus brought her there, and the program paid for it and her medication but she was always alone. The burden was left on her shoulders, except for the small moments I had with her.

"She'd gotten worse the last time I saw her. She started hurting herself." My breathing is ragged and I lean my head against the wall, closing my eyes and willing the images to go away.

"She needed more help than I could give her." There wasn't a phone call I didn't make. Marie became my priority, but I had no rights to her. I had no legal way to protect her or to take her like I so desperately wanted to.

"She's gone?" he asks me.

I wipe the tears away and take a steadying breath. When I lick my lips, the salt coats the tip of my tongue. It's only then that I come back to the moment, to what I can change. To what I can prevent.

"Her death affected me very deeply because it reminded me of-" I hesitate and swallow before I say, "Jay."

John shifts uncomfortably in the steel chair and the metal legs scratch the floor. "Because his father abused him?" he asks.

I'm careful about answering, but I decide to ask, "What do you know about what he did?"

John glances at the red light for a moment, as if distracted by it before looking back at me. "Jay has told me a lot," John answers with a tone that tells me he's uncomfortable.

"Did he tell you his father liked to see how much pain Jay could take before screaming for his dead mother?" The words slip out of me like a void. The brutality and tragedy seeming cold as ice on my lips. I look up into John's eyes as I explain, "It wasn't good enough unless his father believed it was genuine." He tortured him in so many ways. As if it were a game and he was simply trying to find the best tool that was most effective. But nothing ever would be. He would never win; he'd never be content.

"Is that what Marie's father did?" John asks, forcing my gaze back to him. To the present. To being in a basement twenty years later, brought back by the one boy I wish I could have saved.

If only I'd known.

"Yes, but that's not why she reminded me of Jay. When I left both of them, I knew they were going to their deaths." My composure crumbles as I state the words as a fact. Because it's so true.

I left Jay, and Marie left me. "Maybe I never deserved to help her," I croak out. Maybe if she'd been in someone else's care, she'd still be alive. That's the thought that keeps me up at night. The thought that made me down an entire bottle of pills in the hopes of ending my own life.

"I'm so sorry that you lost Marie, Robin," John says with such sympathy as he leans forward that it breaks me. "It's not your fault," he tells me as if it's a truth.

"I knew and I couldn't do anything. And when I left Jay-" My throat closes and refuses to let me take in a breath. My upper body collapses, and I hug my legs close.

Watching her walk away from me was every bit the same as when Jay turned his back on me in the field. He pushed me forward and said he'd stay behind for only a minute, but I knew it.

I knew it would be the last time.

And I still ran.

Marie never gave me the choice.

"Hush," I hear John say at the same time as I hear the bed creak with movement. I focus on calming myself as John rests a large hand on my back and slowly moves it up and down my back in soothing strokes.

His touch makes everything seem like it really will be okay. Like it's not my fault.

"It's alright," he whispers quietly into my ear. I creep closer to him, taking a chance to reach out and grab onto his other arm. And he lets me, he easily scoops me up and puts me in his lap. His arms wrap around me like they belong there, and it soothes something deep inside of me to be held by him.

"I've got you," he whispers and his hot breath sends a chill from my left shoulder all the way down my body. I let out a gentle moan and desire stirs between my legs. I just want to *feel* something other than this.

With him.

"Could you hold me close and stay with me?" I whisper my plea. Always afraid of being denied. "Please," I beg him when he doesn't answer immediately.

My heart stutters and flips as John slides me off his lap and leaves me. I nearly cling to him, I almost reach up to do just that, to grip onto his shirt and beg him to give me another chance, but I know better.

I watch as he walks to the door, leaving me breathing heavily and alone as the sound of it opening and then shutting again signals he's really gone.

My body trembles as I stare at the comforter, rocking on my own and focusing on the one loose thread. When a click fills the silent room and the door slowly opens, I chance a look up.

"Jay," I say and swallow thickly. I'm only slightly relieved when he nods at me. I close my eyes and let the wave of gratitude take over.

"Little bird," he says and his voice is so full of pain.

"Jay, please," I beg him, not caring how I look or how miserably I've failed him today. "I promise I'll do better, but please."

"This is for you too," he tells me softly as he walks to the bed and stops in front of me. I sit there on my knees, looking up at him as though he's my savior. "It's for all of us," he tells me, and it shatters my heart.

"Just hold me," I beg him although my voice comes out strong.

"It's too early to sleep." The memories of him denying me with that excuse rush back. It was always when he'd come back shaken. That's when he wouldn't hold me. It wasn't about me though; it was about him. His arms may have been the ones that wrapped around my body, but the comfort was meant for him. I can't accept that now. Not right now. I need him too much.

"I don't want to sleep; I just want you to hold me." I remember what he said last night, and it makes the pain that much deeper. "Please, Jay. You can hurt me if you want, I deserve it."

Instantly he pulls me into his chest, holding me closer and tighter than John did. Harder even. "Shh," he tries to calm me. "You aren't responsible."

"You needed me," I whisper against his chest. But I close my sore eyes and just allow him to calm me, rocking me side to side. Soothing me in a way no one else ever can.

"It was an impossible situation, Robin." He kisses my hair again like he did last night, and it makes a warmth spread through my chest. My fingers dig into my thighs, keeping me from reaching up to him.

"If you hadn't left, we wouldn't be here now, would we?" he tells me softly as he pets my hair with long strokes. It's relaxing, lulling me to sleep until he adds, "It's fate. Things are meant to happen a certain way."

I shake my head, hating his explanation and wanting to shove his hand away, but knowing not to reach up. *Fate*. Fate would mean Marie was meant to die.

"Please hold me," I beg him and it reminds me of the first time he ever held me. The first time we both knew we needed each other too desperately to ignore. Before I can add that I'll take the consequences, whatever they may be, he lies on the bed, making it dip and groan with his weight.

"For a minute," Jay says and my heart hurts all over again. But at least I have one minute. Just one to hold on to him.

CHAPTER 18

Jay

Twenty years ago

"*If I made a deal with her, do you think she'd hit you?*" *my father asks me as I sit in the steel chair across the room from him. My body shakes from the cold. My clothes are soaked, and the tips of my fingers are numb.*

A deal... is he finally going to let her go?

"*I think she would. She wants to leave more than anything,*" *he says more to himself than to me. I'm afraid to look at him. Afraid that if I do, he'll tell her to do it.*

My little bird.

She's the only good thing in my world. The only purpose I have in life.

Do I think she'd strike me?

Yes.

She'd do anything to leave, and the thought shreds me. I could see him over her shoulder, whispering promises of freedom if only she'll listen to him. Just like he did to me for so long.

"Are you letting her go?" I ask him, and the words tremble from my lips.

A rough dry laugh fills the small chamber as he throws a towel at me. It's small and thin, but it's something. I keep my movements slow as he paces, still not looking him in the eyes. One day I'll be stronger than him. One day I'll kill him for what he's done.

But he likes to show me how weak I am, and he's right. I'm no one compared to him.

The rough towel drags over my skin, drying it as he says, "No, of course not."

He clears his throat, and I chance a look up at him as he stares at the back wall. He turns to look at me ever so slowly, and holds my gaze. My own eyes stare back at me. "She's too important, boy. And I have so many plans for her."

His words echo in my head, over and over. Through the screaming of the next session, through the sound of my feet pattering on the cold floor as he takes me back to her.

I only know two things to be true.

If she leaves, I'd rather kill myself than live another day.

And I need to get her out of here.

I promise I'll find a way out.

I WAKE UP TO MY HEART RACING AND MY BODY FEELING LIKE ice. I stay still, perfectly motionless with my body tense. There's a thin layer of cold sweat covering me. The nightmares always feel so real. Like it just happened. Like I was back with him, helpless and stuck in that fucking chamber. It's only after a moment of calming my breathing that I feel her warmth as she stirs beside me.

My little bird. For a moment it makes me feel like I'm back there again, back in the room and I'm quick to look around. But we're on a bed, a comfortable one with sheets and a blanket. She's with me though; she came down here to sleep with me.

I open my eyes and peek at Toby, fast asleep by the open door. He's huddled in a ball and even he didn't wake this time. I turn over onto my side and pull her small body closer to me. I kiss the crook of her neck and look up, staring at the wall and the camera. It's off, but it's there, staring back at me.

Not only watching me, but it's watching her, too.

I don't want her here at night. It's too real with her in my arms. I whisper into the stale air, loving the feel of her soft body in my arms, "I'll always protect you, little bird."

The moment the words leave me, Robin stirs next to me, opening her weary eyes. They're still red-rimmed from earlier, and I know she's tired. No one is sleeping in this house. I give her a worn out smile and push the hair from her face.

"You left me," she whispers. I shake my head, denying it. Never. I'll never leave her. The accusation in her voice mixed with pain is a heavy cocktail, and I don't want to carry the burden.

"I'm right here," I tell her and when I do, a small smile tugs her lips up just slightly. It softens me and warms my chest. But then she reaches up. I'm quick to snatch her wrists. Quick to stop her. I can't help the reaction. I know it's part of my fucked up head. How once I didn't have my father to fight anymore, I found myself consumed with the past and tearing myself apart instead.

"I want to touch you," she tells me softly, and I stay perfectly still. She can help me. She wants to help me, and I desperately need it. I need her.

My fingers dig into the mattress, and I have to close my eyes as her hands slowly slide up my shirt.

"You're the only one I've let touch me," I tell her in a soft voice.

It was years ago, back when giving her everything was all I had left.

"It would have been different," I start to say, but my voice gets choked. The anger starts to rise, and my blood heats. I close my eyes, breathing out slowly.

It's not her fault, I tell myself. I knew what I was doing when I set her free. But knowing how it all played out... I can't help but feel animosity.

"Punish me, Jay," I hear her soft plea and it forces my eyes open. "Please," she begs me.

I hate how weak she sounds in this moment. I don't want that for her, and I quickly silence her before she can do it again. I crash my lips against hers, spearing my fingers through her hair and parting her lips to deepen the kiss. She obeys me instantly, arching her neck and digging her fingers into my thigh. Letting me know she's not going to move them.

I don't mind her being weak for me. But not when it's tinged with guilt.

She moans into my mouth, and my dick instantly hardens. I rock it into her, needing to feel something. A voice hisses in the back of my head, *mine*, as I break the heated kiss and catch my quickened breath.

"Punish me, Jay," Robin begs me in a whisper laced

with desire. Her eyes are still closed as she waits for my answer.

"Would it make you feel better?" I ask her as I press my chest against hers and slowly let go of her wrists. "If I took it out on you?" I whisper the question, feeling the heat between our bodies mingle with our breath. I slide my fingers along her collarbone and then to the thin silk strap of her nightgown. I don't stop, my touch forcing the strap down her shoulder, letting it fall and exposing her left breast.

My cock is impossibly hard as I stare down at her gorgeous skin, trailing my finger over every inch and watching with bated breath as goosebumps follow my path.

Her pale rosy nipples are already hard as I reach down and pinch one with my forefinger and thumb, pulling back slightly and making her head fall back. A moan slips through her lips, and it forces precum to leak from my cock.

I've wanted her for so long, I know I have, but the anger has kept me from reaching out to her, from touching her. I harbor so much resentment for the day she left that I've feared this moment just as much as I've desired it.

"Jay," she whimpers my name as she shudders, and it's my breaking point. The last restraint I have snaps. I tear the nightgown off her body. The fabric comes apart with a loud rip, accompanied by her gasp.

She wants me to punish her. I will.

She wants me to have her. I'll take every piece of her and leave her with nothing. Nothing without me from this day forward.

I shove my hand between her thighs and her panties are already soaking wet. She writhes under me as I nip her neck and work my hand over her panty-covered cunt, pressing my palm to her swollen nub and ruthlessly forcing her first orgasm from her.

She doesn't expect the first release; it comes quickly and rocks through her body. As the ripples leave her lying limp, I tear through the thin lace and spread her legs for me. I kick off my jeans and boxers and stroke my thick cock just once.

I don't even hesitate. I'm not gentle; I don't give her a chance to acclimate. I thrust into her, slamming my hips to hers and taking her in one swift motion.

Her back bows and she screams out, but I'm quick to press my chest and lips to hers. It calms her as I pull nearly all the way out, feeling her opening at the tip of my cock and then shoving myself all the way back in. She's already wet and hot for me, making it that much easier for me to fuck her so ruthlessly.

I pound into her over and over again, feeling her tight walls spasm around my cock. Each hard thrust is met with a whimper escaping her lips. Her sharp nails digging into my back only spur me to fuck her harder, faster.

I take her with a punishing force, relentlessly pistoning my hips.

Even as she cums on my dick again, so hot and tight and sucking my dick in further, begging for my cum, I refuse. I groan into her neck, grinding my teeth and digging my blunt nails into the flesh at her hips to keep my release from surfacing.

She screams out my name over and over, but I stay still, holding my breath and ignoring the tingling at the base of my spine. My toes curl and my balls draw up, but I deny it. I stay as still as I can, buried deep in her tight cunt until her orgasm passes.

And then I do it again.

And again.

I spread her wider and fuck her deeper and harder each time. Letting the waves of her orgasms build and crash through her, leaving her limp and destroyed each and every time. Her breathing is ragged as she arches her neck and pleads with me.

"Please, Jay," she moans and her voice is a strangled cry. Her words barely audible. A cold sweat forms over every inch of my skin as I ride through her words, not letting up. Her body tries to roll away, in a desperate effort to leave me and I grip her throat tightly in my hand, squeezing as I piston my hips between her legs, forcing her small breasts to bounce. Forcing her hands up to clutch at my wrist. Forcing little cries of pained pleasure from her lips.

"Please what?" I ask her as her lips part with the need to breathe. Her fingernails just barely scratch at my hand, but she doesn't try to pull it away. It's only to make this last one the most intense. To shatter her completely and intensify it so that she'll be more than ruined.

"Please," she tries to speak, but the threat of another orgasm creeps up through her body, making her arch and writhe. As the silent scream is met with her body going stiff, her heels digging into the mattress, I pump my hips

147

again and again, bottoming out against her cervix until my dick pulses and I relent.

I loosen my grip on her throat, listening to her gasp for air and scream my name with nothing but pleasure. My own orgasm finally tears through me, demanding its own relief and forcing her name from my lips. I whisper it in the crook of her neck, her hot breath on my face making my entire body chill.

Our mixed arousal and cum leaks between us as we both catch our breath. And I fall to the mattress next to her sated and mesmerized by the way she lies there panting for air. The way her eyes are dazed and her body trembles. Because of what I've done to her. Because of what I've given her.

She whimpers and tries to move when she realizes I've left her, but I merely splay a hand on her hip and she stills, waiting for me to tell her what to do next.

Her thighs scissor slightly, simply because I've put my hand on her but it's met with a small cry and her brow furrowing.

I lean over her, kissing her gently on the lips before pulling the covers up and around her.

"Don't leave me, please," my little bird begs me, and it destroys every bit of me.

"I won't," I lie to her just to ease her worry. "I'll be right here when you wake up."

CHAPTER 19

Robin

*H*e couldn't help but leave me.

It's all I could think while I stood in the hot stream of water.

I run my fingers through my damp hair as I sit on the bed in the basement.

I'm not sure if John is coming or not. I haven't seen him since he left me yesterday, but it seems fitting to wait for him here. At least one of them will come.

I was foolish enough to think when the bathroom door creaked open and the hot steam drifted away from me that it was Jay, but it was only Toby. Hours later and still no sign of Jay.

My heart splinters as I cross my legs, and I have to close my eyes because of the aching reminder of last night. It was everything I thought it would be and more, but now I'm left alone, just like I was this morning.

I pull the lone pillow on the bed into my lap and lean

against the wall, staring at the door. What a good little victim I'm being for him. My stomach sinks and my mouth dries up. I stay where I'm told to and spread my legs for him, begging him to ruin me.

I close my eyes and turn away from the closed door as Toby whines on the other side.

Jay's not the only one fucked up in the head.

I'm so busy wallowing that I don't hear John come in. It's not until he clears his throat and the door shuts with a thud that I realize he's here now. The air is tense and awkward between us, and I instantly wonder if he knows.

"There you are," he says and attempts a pleasant smile but he fails. "How are you feeling today?" he asks me cautiously, striding to the camera to turn it on and then fiddling with it as if there's anything new to focus on. I think it's just so he doesn't have to look at me.

"Used," I tell him flatly, watching for his reaction. He stills for a moment and my heart beats faster, but then he moves to the chair, the blinking red light greeting me as John takes a seat and the metal legs scrape and produce that irritating sound.

"Are you okay?" he asks me, leaning forward. It's feigned concern. He doesn't mean it. The realization makes tears prick the backs of my eyes, and I hold the pillow tighter.

"Why do you care?" I ask him out of anger. My words are shaky, and I use my middle finger to wipe under my eyes. I won't cry over this. I refuse to.

"Robin," John says my name with sympathy and compassion before rising from the chair and quickly coming to the bed. "Did he hurt you?" he asks me, and I simply shake my head. He rests a hand on my back, but he's holding back.

"You don't-" I try to speak, but my words are muted by the lump in my throat. "I'm hurt because I feel as though I don't matter to you." I tell him the truth, the raw honesty cutting me deeply. He doesn't even remember me. My eyes water at the thought, and I wish I were stronger. I take in a steadying breath and focus on him. How much he needs me.

"Do you like me, John?" I ask him. "Do you think if things were different, that you would like me?" The question carries a heavy weight to it. He has the ability to break me and crush me into a million pieces. I need him as much as I need Jay.

"Of course I do," John answers although he doesn't hold my gaze. I close my eyes, feeling my body turn cold and nausea stir in the pit of my stomach. The way his voice is tense, the 'it's-not-me-it's-you' tone is there. It feels like a breakup. I struggle to breathe for a moment while he speaks, but this is all my fault. I know better than this. It's Jay who makes me weak and stupid, who left me feeling like this. But I knew it would end like this. I'm the one who pushed.

"Yesterday, when I left-" he stops to rub the back of his neck and lets out an uneasy sigh. "I don't know how to handle this, Robin. You're fragile, and this situation-"

I cut him off and say, "It's intense, but I-" I ball up my hands in frustration and scoot away from his touch. "I need you to know that what you think of me is very important to me." I swallow thickly and gauge his reaction.

"What I think doesn't matter," John answers, shaking his head slightly.

"It does, John." I reach out slowly and risk placing my fingers in his hand, and that small touch is what breaks down his walls.

He wraps his strong hand around mine and sits closer to me on the bed, scooting back and licking his lips before looking up at me.

I can feel my eyes widen as I wait with bated breath for the truth. I can tell that's what he's going to say. "I feel for you," he says, and my heart thumps. "I feel a very strong urge to protect you, and to..." He trails off and waves a hand in the air as if he's looking for the right word.

"You don't have to sugarcoat it, John," I tell him as I keep my composure.

He looks back at me with an intensity that shocks me.

"This is fucked up," he tells me in a lowered voice, his eyes lightening as he says, "What I want to do to you is even worse."

I have to break his gaze and I stare at my fingers as I pull my hand away from his and grip the sheet on the mattress. I take a chance and peek at him. "What do you want to do to me?" I ask him.

"I want to take you away and keep you," he says, and a warmth flows through my body. He leans forward and I think he's going to kiss me, but he doesn't. Instead he puts his lips close to my ear and whispers, "I want to fuck you until you forget. Until you're only mine."

I close my eyes at his admission.

He backs away, and the chill from the basement air breaks the moment we had.

"But you're in love with Jay, and there's something between you two. I don't have a place interfering."

He's so wrong. So, fucking wrong. I part my lips to tell him just that, but as he sits back on the bed, straightening his shoulders, I see the blinking light.

Always watching.

I have to be careful. I have to tell John, but it would be so much easier if he could just remember.

CHAPTER 20

John

Days pass easily, each one bleeding into the next. She's addictive. The sound of her soft voice and the even cadence when she tells me stories charm me.

But they're about her and Jay. What her life was like before and after.

About missing him and how she could never forget what they went through.

What shreds me is her guilt, the way she describes moving on with her life as though it's a confession. It shouldn't be that way, but it doesn't matter how many times I tell her. That pained look in her eyes only gets worse.

The fluorescent light above my head flickers, and I look up to watch it. These sessions aren't moving things forward, and doing them in the basement is only aggravating me more and more.

"Is everything okay?" Robin's soft voice calls to me from across the room. She's on the bed as usual, her heels propped up as she hugs her legs, leaning back against a pillow with her head against the wall.

I clear my throat and glance at the camera, the red light blinking and wonder if Jay even watches. He doesn't ask about them in the least.

"What do you want to gain from this, Robin?" I ask her, my heart rate climbing. It's obvious she has no intention of leaving. What's happened between her and Jay has touched them both deeply, but I'm a conflicting factor. Every day it gets harder to leave. Every day I grow jealous. I get angrier.

This isn't the man I am. I need to get the fuck out of here.

"I want to know more about you, John," she answers me after taking a moment. She seems nervous as she watches for my reaction.

She wants me. I can fucking feel it, and I want her too. It only makes the situation that much more fucked up.

"What do you want to know?" I ask her, crossing my ankle over my knee and rubbing the rough stubble on my jaw with my thumb.

"Tell me about growing up?" she asks. It's an innocent question, but the look on her face is so serious. As if the answer will affect her deeply.

"There's not much to me," I tell her and sit back. "My story isn't like yours or Jay's." A sigh leaves me as I rub the back of my neck and look at the door.

"Tell me about your parents," Robin offers and my eyes flick to hers. I watch how she picks at the comforter as if her idle hands need to be taking notes. It makes me smile and reminds me there's so much more to her than the past she has with Jay. It also reminds me that she's probably used to this. Being the questioner and not the questionee.

"I was adopted when I was younger. And I was visiting the orphanage when I met Jay." The hint of a smile on my face vanishes at the memory. "My parents were young and they did what they thought was best when they gave me up, but Jay…" I can't finish the thought. He needed someone so badly. I saw how everyone looked at him. How they judged him.

I clear my throat and rub my palms on my jeans. "Anyway." I tell her the basic rundown. "I did alright in school, B student mostly. I wasn't really interested. I guess I was kind of quiet."

"And you're a mechanic?" Robin asks, and I nod my head.

"Yeah, I've always loved working on cars and bikes. It made sense." I nod my head and remember the shop just sitting there, but the bills aren't going away. "I enjoy working for myself but the downsides are the long hours and the lack of socializing."

"Are you a social butterfly?" Robin asks with a bit of humor. A rough laugh rumbles up my chest as I shake my head.

"Never really been into crowds," I answer her honestly.

"Not a lot of friends?" she asks.

"I'm not a loner like Jay," I answer her, feeling defensive. "A few guys work for me at the shop and we hang out occasionally. I can take them or leave them. I guess I'm a bit of a loner after all." I hadn't realized it until she questioned me. The bartender at the local pub and Steve a mechanic looking for part-time work are my two closest friends. And of course Jay.

"I'm a loner," Robin says, interrupting my thoughts. "I'm very much alone." She gives me this sad smile.

"Why's that?" I ask her. She shouldn't be alone ever. I could talk to her for hours and hours every day and be content with nothing else. She's the type of person you feel like you already know before she even lays eyes on you. She should definitely never be alone.

"I don't know why," she tells me and then looks down at the sheet. She stretches her back and then asks me, "Do you like to be alone at night?"

"Not in particular," I answer without thinking about anything other than her company in the evening. "I wouldn't mind company at night," I say and my blood heats as she holds my gaze and fire sparks between us.

"Why do you leave at night?" she asks me like it's a sin.

My brow furrows, and the pit of my stomach fills with guilt. "Do you want me to stay?" I ask her.

Her eyes search mine for a minute, as if she's not sure of the right answer. It fucking guts me.

"You love Jay?" I ask her, changing the subject and putting the attention back onto her. I know she does. It's why I can never have her. Why I feel compelled to carry on with this charade.

"I do," she says and my blood turns to ice. It's one more reason I need to leave. When I peek back up at her, she looks as though she's going to cry. It happens almost every day. When she breaks down and holds back from me.

I hate it. It keeps me coming back to her because I want to be the one to help her. The one she leans on. *The one she leaves with.*

I know I should tell her that it's okay. That it's natural to love him. That he loves her, too. But those aren't the words that come out of my mouth.

"I really hate that you get so upset. I just want to help you so you can move past this." *So she can get away from Jay.* I keep the thought to myself, but it's true. I want to keep her far away from him. But right now, she feels she needs him. She feels *for* him.

"Then help me, John," she says with a strained voice. Like she's so close, yet so far away.

"Tell me what you need," I tell her. And I mean it. I don't want her to be upset or hurt in any way. She's a strong, beautiful woman who should be happy. The past is where it's supposed to be, and she should know she deserves happiness.

"I need you to remember," she whispers and stares deep into my eyes.

"Remember what?" I ask her, my heart beating slow and my body heating. It's fear that keeps me still. Fear that I'm somehow involved in what happened all those years ago. I've tried so many times to think back to how I know this woman, but nothing comes to mind.

I must though, because she calls to me in a way I can't deny.

She gives me a small smile, but it's sad. Everything about her is a beautiful shade of sadness. "Can you tell me what you know of me again?" she asks me.

I sit back with slight relief, but the feeling that I'm

failing her is so heavy on my chest I can't speak. "Can you tell me how we first met?" she asks me. Pushing me.

I try to answer her, I try to think but my memory is so hazy.

"Do you want to talk about something else?" she asks me, breaking up the throbbing headache and the over-whelming anxiety. Her hazel eyes shine with sincerity. "I just want to talk to you," she tells me and leans against the wall.

She's obviously lying, and it's then that it hits me.

This session isn't about her.

I'm not here to help her at all.

I'm not meant to interview her.

Jay set me up.

These sessions are all about me.

CHAPTER 21

Robin

$\mathcal{I}$'m done sleeping alone. Or trying to, rather. Every second that passes is like a ticking bomb and I need to be close to him when it goes off. That, and I can't fucking sleep. Not without him.

It's been days.

Days of walking on eggshells and finding our footing. But we know who we are and what we want. And I'm tired of waiting.

The moment my heels hit the plush rug, Toby yawns at the door and stretches. He doesn't stand as I cautiously walk to the door, but his eyes are on me. He's slow to stand and make sure I don't go to the front door. That and the basement exit are the only two doors that set him off. Any other time, he simply follows me like a guardian rather than a warden. "It's funny that you used to scare me, you know?" I tell the dog as he looks up at me with the widest puppy eyes. I know there's a beast inside of him that could rip me limb from limb. I'm well aware of that fact. But the animal refusing to leave my side is just a big puppy dog.

I bend down and pat his head as he walks with me although my heart is racing.

I don't think Jay will deny me like he did the first night and if he does, I'm going to fight him on that. I don't think it will come to that though. He doesn't want to deny me, just as I don't want to refuse him of anything.

We need progress, not perfection, I think as I head to the bedroom across from the basement door. I don't try to be quiet at all. I want him to know I'm not sneaking around or trying anything.

The door's wide open and filled with so much more light than my own room. It's only moonlight, but the blinds are open and they send stripes of shadows across the bed. They lay on Jay's bare thighs and chest and all the way up to his chin.

I stop in the doorway, the floors creaking as I take in a steadying breath.

"You should be sleeping," Jay says without turning to look at me. Toby yawns again then arches his back before circling in the hallway behind me. The sound of his paws and the jingle of his tag are so loud. I swallow thickly, ripping my eyes away from him and taking a step into Jay's bedroom.

"I thought you slept downstairs," I tell him and he finally turns to look at me, although the rest of his body is still.

"It's different, knowing you're up here." His eyes travel down my body slowly, assessing me. The way his eyes heat creates an instant tension in the room that makes me shift slightly, ignoring the way my core heats. Jay has a power over me that's undeniable.

I walk toward the bed and sit down on the edge as I talk. "I think that's a good thing. It's change, and change is good."

My hands rest in my lap as I wait for him to respond. His eyes narrow, and he's quiet for a long time.

"Why aren't you sleeping?" he asks me, although he already knows the answer.

My throat gets tight as I scoot further into his bed and my knee brushes his. "I want to sleep with you," I push the words out and then look Jay in the eyes.

Slowly, ever so slowly, a smile tugs at his lips.

"Please?" I ask him and he hesitates but then shakes his head.

"You can't be here when John comes," he says although there's no conviction in his voice.

I ignore him and simply pull the sheet and comforter down and crawl into bed.

"You're getting bold, Robin," Jay says with a bit of an admonishment, but then he wraps his arm around me and pulls me closer to him. "I love it," he says with a soft smile.

I smile into his chest and then look up at him.

The faint light of the moon filtering in through the windows highlights the sharp lines of his jaw and his rough stubble. I nudge my nose against his chin and he lets out a huff of a laugh.

"You really should be sleeping," he tells me and I nuzzle next to him. I wish I felt warm fuzzy feelings, but I don't. I feel nothing but anxiety.

"I want to talk," I tell him and it makes him laugh. A genuine laugh that's rough and bubbles up from his chest. It's the sweetest sound to hear, and it reminds me of the first time I heard it. Pure joy from a man so devoid of any happiness.

"Of course you do." He runs a hand down his face and lets out an easy sigh before looking at me. "What do you want to talk about, little bird?"

"Anything," I answer him. "Just tell me something." I nestle closer to him, but keep my hands to myself. I love this. This easiness and openness. I want this forever.

"I feel better now with you," he tells me and it makes me smile, but the happiness quickly vanishes. "Before I thought it would be better if I just left." He looks into my eyes as he talks, absently trailing his fingers over the dip in my waist.

"I thought it would be easier if I was just gone."

"That's a horrible thought to have, Jay and you're so wrong-"

"Shh," Jay shushes me and calms me down by kissing my forehead. "I know that. I could never leave you anyway. Even if you had no idea I was there."

His admission only makes me feel that much worse. "I wish I'd been there for you," I whisper against his chest. I desperately want to rest my hand against his chest, but instead I move my fingers to the front of his pajama bottoms and slip them just over the edge so I'm comfortable.

"I can't tell you how many nights I wanted to get in bed with you," Jay says. "I know it's wrong. Stalking or whatever, but I wanted it. I wanted to go after you."

"I wish you had. I wish you hadn't waited."

"It's not like I could have shown up and asked you out for coffee." Jay huffs a chuckle, and it makes my body shake. His large arm wraps around me. "I wish things were different. I wish I wasn't broken for you." The smile vanishes as he rubs his eyes and lets out a heavy sigh.

"*We're* broken," I correct him. I chew on the inside of my lip, thinking about how to word the next question. The one thing that's really kept us apart.

"Have you tried to tell John at all?" I ask him and stay perfectly still, staring at the bedroom wall.

"He hates me," Jay says as if it's a fact.

"He doesn't."

"There's hate behind the pity. It's why he doesn't want to know," he says and it makes my heart clench.

"Can we talk about something else, little bird?" Jay asks and then kisses my forehead. "Or sleep?"

"He's the only thing holding us back," I tell him. I need more. I know I can't push, but I want Jay in my life fully and completely and I need more than this.

"Us?" he asks.

"Don't pretend, Jay. I won't let you do it, too," I say and there's a strength to my voice I don't recognize. I add, "I love you too much."

I want so desperately for him to say the words back to me. I want to hear it although I feel it deep in my soul already. I want him to acknowledge it more than anything.

It's quiet for a long moment. My breathing steadies and my eyes drift shut as I listen to the sound of his steady heartbeat and sink deeper into his comforting warmth.

"Do you love him too?" he asks me quietly a moment later.

I don't answer his question. I can't. Because right now, I know if I tell him the truth, it will break him. And I'll never hurt Jay. Never.

CHAPTER 22

Robin

*I*t's not snooping if you're looking for something that will help a person you love.

I'm sure that's what parents say when they're searching their children's rooms and going through their text messages. I need to find something, anything that could show John the truth. Something that's irrefutable.

I'm sure all the evidence is burned and left in ashes, but that doesn't stop me from opening one drawer and then the next in Jay's bedroom.

If only I could find something. The thought makes my heart twist with pain. I don't want to be the one to show him. I don't want to be there when he's forced to face who he is. It's going to ruin him, but only then will all of us be able to heal.

The sound of the floor creaking makes my eyes whip up to the door, my heart racing. They travel down to Toby and I nearly smile looking at him stretch his back.

An easy sigh leaves me, but then I jump at the sight of John.

I put a hand over my heart and try not to look guilty as I push the drawer back in. I didn't find a damn thing. Jay isn't one to keep things. Nothing worth any sentimental value. Nothing that reminds him of his past.

"Robin," John says my name low, as if he's afraid someone will hear him. Jay.

"What's wrong?" I ask him as my blood chills and my throat gets tight. "Is everything alright?"

"I think we need to leave, Robin." I nod my head once, thinking maybe I could convince him to go to the hospital, but he's not in the right mindset. He wouldn't believe a damn thing if I told him the truth.

I take a hesitant step toward John as he talks, "We can get out of here. I'll take you home or ...to my place?" he asks as if it's a question. Like I'd need protection from Jay.

He has no idea it's him who I need to protect myself from. "John," I say and his name comes out like a plea.

"I know you feel guilty," John starts and I shake my head, turning away from him to look out of the window. I cross my arms, feeling trapped. Not by the solid walls, not by the men I love, but by my past. And hasn't it always been like that?

"It's not about that," I tell him honestly. "I can't go now. I see why Jay did this. Why he wants it this way."

I turn back to face John, and his expression has fallen. He's leaving. I've failed them both.

I reach out for his hand and he takes it before telling me, "I can't do this anymore, Robin; I need you to come with me."

His thumb rubs back and forth over my wrist with a soothing rhythm. I lick my lips and look deep into his eyes as I tell him, "I don't want you to go."

"You're not okay. I can see that you feel like you have an obligation to him. You love him, I get that, but this isn't right."

An uneasy breath leaves me as I watch every little move John makes. My lips part, but my voice is silent. I swallow thickly and refuse to let go of his hand when he starts to pull away.

"Can we go outside?" I ask him. I just need to feel like I can breathe.

He simply nods and walks beside me, not letting go of my hand, but not attempting to get closer either.

"I felt like we were making progress," I tell him and watch Toby as we get to the front door. It's a large heavy door made of solid wood and stained a dark brown. Toby doesn't have a problem in the least as John opens it. He almost closes the door right after him, but Toby slips out with us, staying close to my side and I've never wanted him more.

I reach down to pet him, feeling as though my breath is strangled. Sometimes progress isn't enough. It's not enough to keep John. It's not enough to ease the burden on Jay's conscience.

A chill sweeps across my skin and goosebumps spread along my arms as I shudder. The fresh air is what I needed though.

"There's a porch," I say with a bit of humor in my voice. I haven't stepped foot outside. It reminds me of the world outside of here. Of the life I used to have. The one we could share together.

John leans against the banister and looks out into the empty field, not looking at me as he tells me, "Jay will be back soon, and I'm going to tell him I'm not coming back here. I'm done with this."

The air gets colder and more tense as my eyes narrow and I watch him. "I thought we were doing better," I tell him although it comes out a question.

He turns to look at me, but quickly looks back out into the field of nothing.

I have to tell him. I have to push. Toby whines as the thought hits me, and I reach down to pet him again. I've never been more scared in my adult life.

I slowly sit, although my legs are shaky and this close to Toby's jaws reminds me of the vicious barking, the way he held me down that first night. I ignore it all. I have to give a piece to John. Something to keep him.

"John, I want to tell you a secret."

"What's that?" he asks and looks down at me, but I don't look back up at him as I pet Toby and try to think of what to tell him. It's been days and I don't know what I can say that he'd believe.

"I knew you when you were a child." My heart hurts as I confess. "This one time, you taught me how to whistle with a blade of grass." The memory is so fresh. I can still feel the bit of sunshine. A reward I was terrified would come with a punishment. "Do you remember?" I ask him.

I take a peek up to look at him, and his expression tells me everything I already knew. He doesn't remember a damn thing, and he won't believe me. All the time we spent together, none of it exists for him.

I hold the tears back as Toby rests his head in my lap. His warmth is so at odds with the bitter coldness that surrounds me.

"Are you alright?" he asks me, and my heart sinks even further.

"You don't remember me, but I'm not lying to you, John." I steady my breath. "I'm not crazy," I tell him and as the words slip out, I feel as though I am. I'm beyond sane at least.

"We never knew each other. The first time I saw you..." John starts, but doesn't finish his sentence. I wait, holding my breath and hoping for something, but also fearing it.

Please remember me. Please, John. I need you.

"You ripped it right out of the ground," I tell him, brushing beneath my nose with my forearm and not giving a damn about it. "And put it right to your lips." A smile forces its way to my lips and a laugh bubbles up. "I thought you were eating it," I tell him.

Silence greets me, and this time I don't look up to gauge his reaction. I let my body sway with Toby.

"I'm not the only one who's hurt, John. Neither is Jay." I whisper the words and half expect him to ask how it relates to Jay. Part of me hopes he will, but he doesn't.

Finally, he says, "I don't remember any of that."

"It's okay," I say and smile weakly. "I mean, I wish you did. I really wish you knew how much you meant to me."

"Then leave with me?" John asks.

"Will you listen if I..." I can't finish. He won't believe me, or worse, it'll push him farther away.

"Robin, whatever Jay told you-"

I shake my head and close my eyes. "This isn't something he told me, John." My voice is hard and unforgiving.

"I love you, John. You don't remember me, but I think you love me, too," I tell him, exposing everything I'm most afraid of. "Just don't leave me. Not yet. Not until I can tell you everything."

CHAPTER 23

Robin

I'm not used to waiting this long. I pick at my nails, wondering if I've ruined everything. Wondering if I should try to find him. I wish there were a clock in here. Something. Anything to fill up the silence.

My eyes drift back to the only constant in the room. The camera that's facing me.

The light isn't on, but it feels like it's taunting me that much more with it off. Like the cameras never mattered. Nothing did. It was going to happen regardless.

I slide off the bed, feeling restless and with an anxiety that won't go away. I hate that camera. I hate the blinking red light. I swallow thickly as I walk toward it. My throat is tight as I remember how the monster's breath felt against my neck like a sticky fog. How my body screamed in pain and the bed shook as he took something from me I could never have back. I stared at the red light through my tears. Watching it blinking and recording everything. Just watching it all happen to me.

And there wasn't a damn thing I could do to stop it.

I stopped screaming, I stopped crying. I had nothing left but the fucking light to take me away.

Pathetic. I'm fucking pathetic. The faint memory flashes before my eyes.

A cry rips through me as my fist swings in the air, slamming against the cold metal of the camera.

Fuck you! Then it crashes to the floor and I scream as I reach down and grab it before cracking it against the unforgiving floor again.

I was never pathetic. My teeth grind together as his face stares back at me. The face of a monster. Nothing but coldness in his eyes.

I hate him. I hate what he did to me and how I can never change it.

I scream out as I pick up the stand and slam it over and over against the broken camera. Small pieces of metal scatter as I recklessly destroy each and every piece I can. My muscles scream and the adrenaline pumps faster and faster, but I've never felt so alive. So liberated.

Jay's father did something to me; he changed me forever. But I won't let him define me. *That* will *never* define who I am.

My shoulders rise and fall with each heavy breath. No more fucking camera. No more of this. I won't do it anymore. I'm done with this shit.

I swallow my nervousness, my hands still trembling as I loosen my grip and let the leg fall to the ground. My body shakes as I look around, but instead of feeling crazed, instead of feeling scared by what I've done, I feel nothing but triumphant.

A creak to my right makes my body jolt.

I turn toward the door as it opens, breathing heavily, feeling invisible and empowered.

"Little bird," Jay tsks, his boots smacking on the cement floor as he makes his way to me. "That wasn't a very nice thing to do," he says with a hint of condescension in his voice. But the corner of his lips curls up into a half smile.

I break his gaze to look at the shattered camera laying in pieces on the ground.

"I fucking hate it," I mutter beneath my breath.

"So you broke it?" he asks me, his voice tinged with surprise. My palms turn sweaty as I look into his eyes, hoping to find approval. He stops in front of me, his broad shoulders and chest at my eye level and dominating me with his presence alone. There's a power about Jay that's undeniable, a confidence and demeanor that won't be denied.

"Yes," I answer him and wait for his reply. Clinging to the hope that he'll understand. It's not just a camera. It's something more. A pain I can't describe. He nods his head once and then looks past me at the pile of broken pieces on the floor.

"It's funny that you break what you hate... yet I seem to be the opposite?" Jay speaks in a riddle, not quite to me, maybe more to himself.

"I didn't mean to," I tell him quickly. "I'm just...,"

"Angry," Jay answers for me.

"Yes," I answer him in a whisper. He takes a step closer

to me, filling in the space between us with heat. His large hands wrap around my hips and I slowly move my hands up to his lower back. Both of us are testing boundaries. My heart beats quickly as I tilt my head up. His hands move down and to my backside. He squeezes my ass and pulls me into him, hard and with a force that makes me gasp.

"It's easy to blame the anger," he says, staring into my eyes. His voice is like a hiss, like a spoken sin. He lowers his lips so they're close to mine, but he doesn't kiss me. "But you and I both know it's more than that. So much more."

I can't take the proximity, the intensity. I don't ask for his permission. I don't wait for him to make the move. I'm taking what I want.

I crash my lips against his and he's quick to react, to deepen it. To lift me up and force my legs to wrap around his hips as he lays me on the bed. His tongue parts the seam of my lips, and I open for him instantly.

Take me. Have me. Do whatever you want with me. I've always been yours.

My breath quickens and my chest rises chaotically as he peels my clothes from me. His fingers slip across my skin with a tenderness that's only thinly hiding the beast of a man Jay is.

His lips kiss and nip my skin, moving over every inch in a torturous fashion. My shoulders dig into the bed as my back arches and he swirls his tongue along my sensitive nipple. His hands, his lips, the roughness of his jeans brushing against my skin. It's all too much.

"Jay," I whimper his name. This is the only way I want

his name to ever come from my lips again. My head is dizzy with desire and it takes a moment before the cool air makes me realize he's on his knees, upright and waiting for my attention. My eyes move slowly, trailing along every hard line of the muscles on his chest and shoulders. He waits to speak until I meet his hungry gaze.

"You want me?" he asks as his deft fingers unbutton his jeans. My eyes are drawn to the movement and I slowly crawl to him as if moving too quickly will make him change his mind.

I nod my head once and whisper in a sultry voice I don't recognize, "Yes, please."

"Take it from me," he tells me as he shoves his pants down. He strokes his cock once and my eyes are drawn to it. I lick my lips and show him my intentions but his hand comes out, pushing my shoulders away.

I look up at him, a wave of denial threatening to steal my happiness, but his thumb brushes against my lips and he says, "If I wanted these fuckable lips I'd tell you. Give me your pussy," he commands.

I can barely breathe as I turn on the mattress, listening to it groan as I get on all fours and reach between my legs for his cock. As I do, he swipes his fingers through my slick folds and brushes my throbbing clit over and over. "You're so fucking wet," he groans and I half expect him to lose control, to take me like he did before. He says it like he's surprised, like I wasn't made for him.

"Please," I whimper and lower my head to the mattress. My fingernails scrape along the sheet. I'm close already. I want him that badly.

The only movement he makes is to gently stroke my

ass. I peek back at him, willing him to take me as ruthlessly and savagely as he wants to.

"Show me how much you want me," he says under his breath as he towers over me, looking down at me with a heat in his eyes I'm sure is mirrored in my own.

In this moment, the only thing that matters is showing him just how much I desire his touch. How much I crave his affection and acceptance. His love.

I want him more than I ever have. More than I've wanted anything else.

I want him more than I want my own life.

CHAPTER 24

John

"What happened to the camera?" I ask Jay as I stand in the opening of the bathroom door. There's still a bit of steam on the bathroom mirror and I watch as he wipes it off with his forearm. He looks over his shoulder at me, his hair still damp from the shower as he puts his t-shirt on over his head.

"The camera?" he asks, turning back to the mirror.

A tick in my jaw twitches as he ignores me. "The fucking camera is destroyed." My blood heats with anger. I'm tired of being a fucking pawn in this game he's playing. And how he likes to ignore me.

"She broke it," he says simply. The mention of *her*, of the sweet woman he's toying with does something to me.

"She did that?" I ask him with an air of disbelief, but also one of pride. She's stronger than she knows. She deserves better, so much better.

The past is the only thing that stands in her way. And that's just what Jay is.

"She fucking loved doing it," he says and there's a sense of pride in his voice and it echoes the jealousy in me. I clear my throat, wishing I could shake it off. Wishing I wasn't caught in between. *Wishing I could just walk away.*

"She's doing better," I say and watch the easiness about him slowly dim as I wait for him to respond.

"She wants you. You know that?" He cocks a brow at me meant to be friendly in nature, but it's not. I know he wants her. He fucking loves her, and she loves him. But I'd take her from him in a heartbeat. I want her just as much as he does. I can love her better. Treat her better. I can give her so much more.

"She should go now," I tell him, ignoring his accusation and the way my blood pumps harder and hotter. I can't look him in the eyes as the vision of having her again and again beneath me flashes before my eyes. *She'd love me more.*

"You want her too," he says, and my eyes flash up to his. "You want to fuck her. Marry her?" he asks me with that same wicked grin on his face. "You want to put a baby in her and ride off into the sunset?" he asks and tilts his head, egging me on.

"I'd give her a better life than you ever could." The words slip between my lips with a menacing growl.

He only laughs at me, then gives a sarcastic grunt and turns back to the mirror. Fucking prick. "You wish you could," he says beneath his breath, gripping the sides of the countertop as his expression hardens. The real him showing. The anger and the hate.

"You're using her," I tell him, feeling the swell of anger rise. I crack my knuckles on my right hand with my thumb, trying to keep from balling it into a fist.

He turns to look at me, waiting for more.

"All you are is using her."

"Maybe." A confident smile stretches across his face, and the danger in his darkened eyes is so apparent, so real. "I am using her. And she fucking loves it."

I can't fucking take it anymore. I love her. I fucking love this woman who's caught in a web of lies and hurt.

Adrenaline pumps through my body, burning up my skin. I hear the pulsing thud of my blood loud in my ears.

I won't let him get away with it. It ends now.

A snarl rips through me as I slam both of my fists into Jay's shoulders, landing hard and knocking into him with all my weight. I'm not used to this aggression. To this all-consuming rage, but when it comes to her, I can't hold it back. She makes me feel a side of me I've never known. She makes me want more. And I want her all to myself.

Jay's a fucking dead man.

He stumbles, smashing his shoulder and head against the bathroom wall. Before he gains his balance, I land a blow into his gut that nearly has him doubling over. But Jay's taken enough punches to know how to handle them. He mutters under his breath, "Motherfucker!" while ramming his shoulder into my gut. My eyes shut tight with the spike of pain that shoots up my body.

My legs lose their balance as my boot backs into the tub, tripping me. I grit my teeth and cling to the shower curtain as it rips the bar down, falling violently with a loud clank into the tub behind me.

I fall hard on my knees and elbows onto the tile with Jay's muscular frame crushing down on mine. I quickly wrap a leg around his calf and push my weight to the opposite shoulder, forcing him down on his back with me landing hard on his chest.

"She's mine," I tell him finally. "I won't let you hurt her," I say although I'm winded. He already has. He's destroyed her and ruined something so beautiful and pure. "I fucking hate you," I seethe at him.

My fist slams into the floor as I try to gain my balance and focus. It hurts like a bitch and splits my knuckles. My left hand grabs the collar of his shirt as I raise my bloodied right fist, eyes focusing on his pretty boy nose.

My breaths come in pants as he plants a punch on my left cheek before I'm able to gain my balance and take a swing at him. *Fuck!* I stagger back, both fists immediately going to my face to block any more punches. I land on my ass, but move to my feet the second I see Jay breathing heavy and struggling to get up.

"I hate you too," he says with a smile. There's blood coating his teeth as he sways in front of me. "I can't tell you enough how much I fucking hate you."

The venom in his voice is all too real, and I feel the same right back.

It's me or him when it comes to Robin. "Between the two of us, she'll choose me. Always," he says as if reading my mind. The smile stays in place as he wipes the blood from his mouth with the back of his hand.

He's right. My heart beats hard at the recognition. She'd choose him. And I can't fucking let it happen. She deserves so much more. Someone better than him.

181

My hands grip around his throat and at first, I feel flesh, real hot flesh that my fingers sink into, but the harder I push, the more I try to choke the life from this bastard, the less it feels real.

My vision shifts and he's no longer in front of me. My fingers are no longer around his throat, but instead on the edge of the mirror.

"Fuck you!" he sneers and he's back, his vicious eyes piercing into me with a threat of death and I smash my forehead against his.

Glass splinters against my forehead, it smashes around me. I hear the crack, I can fucking feel it, but when I open my eyes, he's there staring back at me. A smile on his face as he bashes his head into mine again and again and again.

A punishing abuse until I'm standing in front of a broken mirror, clinging to the edges of it and his image fades, leaving only my reflection.

My heart races, and my head's dizzy with pain throbbing and shooting through me.

CHAPTER 25

John

Twenty years ago

"Come on," I say and my voice is low. So low. I can't speak any louder, but she's moving so slow. I'm afraid he'll hear us. The keys jingle if I hold her hand. But I can't let go of her.

My heart races, beating uncontrollably at the thought of what will happen if he catches us. If he finds out that we're trying to escape.

He'll kill us. I know he will. He'll definitely kill my little bird. I can't let that happen. I turn back to look at her over my shoulder.

Her heels dig in and scrape against the cement as she resists me, and her fingernails scratch at my wrist to let her go.

"We need to go now," I tell her in a stern voice and her face crumples with fear. She shakes her head and her dirtied hair barely moves. Her eyes are wide with fear as she tells me, "We can't."

Her shoulders hunch when she hears the vicious barking of the dogs. "Close the door," she begs me, but I refuse.

I can hear him banging on the door. I can hear my father screaming. I'm surrounded by threats, threats that are promises for me, but empty for her.

"Right now, Robin," I say and grip her chin in my hand and look her in the eyes. "It's now or never," I tell her in a soft voice. My heart pains in my chest. Like nails scraping it slowly, shredding it piece by piece.

"I'm dead," I tell her. "If I stay, I'm dead." I only say those words for her. There's no other choice for me.

I've locked my father in the cellar. He's arrogant to think I could never slip by him. I only have one chance though. And as he rattles the door and screams at me, I nearly cower in front of her. I'm dead when he gets out, and I know he will.

The dogs I have a plan for, but she needs to go the opposite way. She needs to run without being followed.

"No, Jay," she cries.

"We need to go now," I tell her again and although the small girl's expression is only one of fear, she grips my hand tightly and finally moves. I don't give her a second chance, or myself one either. Every step is one more step away from losing her forever. One more step toward my death.

But it's for her. And it's worth it.

My life is so meaningless, but this gives me something.

I have to tug her wrist as we run up the cellar steps.

The dogs are just outside the kitchen in the crate. The gate is closed, but they can get out. They have before. The lock on it isn't much at all. I'll have to hold it if I can't find anything to shove between the handles and strengthen the lock.

I stare out of the kitchen door only for a moment, knowing it's time to say goodbye.

"Jay, what do we do?" she asks me in a strangled voice.

"You need to run first, little bird." I stare at the dogs as they snarl and I tell her, "You have to go first. Straight through the field and into the woods. Keep going straight." I ignore her as she objects.

There's a road, it's a dirt road, but I've seen cars go by on it more than once. "Follow the road and I'll be right behind you," I lie to her.

I turn my back to the dogs and face her, managing a smile. How that's possible, I don't know. The tears in her eyes make me feel weak. Like I've failed her, but this is all I can offer.

I wish I had more.

"Promise me, you'll run no matter what you hear?" I ask her and it only makes her more scared. I hate myself for doing this to her, but it's the only way I know.

At the sound of the cellar doors smashing open in the basement beneath us, I quickly turn, gripping her wrist and pulling her with me as I rip the kitchen door open and yell at her to run.

***

. . .

CLUNK, THE SOUND IS SO SHARP. SO CRYSTAL CLEAR. THE pain from the excruciating hit immediate, but also numbing.

I open my eyes and see my father. The memory flashes in my vision over and over. I'm on the ground, my hands in the mix of dirt and grass. It's so cold.

She's gone. She's safe. She left me.

My head falls back, and I cry. For the first time in so long, I cry without the tears being forced at the hands of my father.

"You fucking prick," my father sneers at me and I back away. Shuffling backward in the grass, the heels of my bare feet digging into the freezing cold mud.

It's not fast enough. No matter how much I'd like to pretend, I'm not bigger than him, not stronger than him.

I'm weak.

I'm only a child.

He raises the shovel up high in the air, and I don't try to block it this time, I don't do anything but sit there in a numb fear with the vision of her running away.

I only got a glimpse before Father came in. The dogs were furious, barking so loud and viciously. But I locked them in. I pushed a stick through the cages. I couldn't breathe until he ran from me to go to them.

In that moment, her foolish wish was also mine. I wanted her to be a bird and fly up so high. High enough that no one could touch her. Not the dogs, not my father.

I only wanted her to be safe.

But then my father came back. He dragged me out here and he's making me watch as he digs the hole.

The shovel raises up high again, and this time something's different. The sharp clunk as it smashes against my head, the hot blood that drips down my forehead.

I can't feel any of it.

It's not me.

My head hurts as I stare down at the boy. My hands can feel the metal in my hand, the wood of the handle as I watch the boy yank it away from the man.

It's not me though.

I stare in horror as he slams the shovel into the man's gut. He's a small boy, like me. He's skinny though, he's dirty. And he's a murderer.

His chest heaves as he beats the man several times with the shovel. Blood splatters on the ground. Over and over, even as the man lies dead and limp, the boy doesn't stop.

The boy is angry, and he's not well. I feel so sorry for him, but I'm too terrified to move.

I stay on the ground and watch as he slowly drags the man to the pit. It's not much, but he's tired and the boy can't do anything other than move the man to the shallow grave.

When he looks up at me, my heart stops. The boy's anger turns to something else, and his eyes narrow.

"Who are you?" he asks me. My heart beats fast and I don't know how to answer him. I don't remember who I am, I only remember my name.

"John," I tell him.

The boy sniffles and looks down at the dead man in the dirt and then back at me, nodding. "I'm not John," he says and it confuses me.

"My name's Jay."

CHAPTER 26

Robin

*M*y heart is racing and won't stop; it's pounding so hard it hurts. My fingers tremble as I push the bathroom door open slowly. It creaks noisily, and I can't even breathe.

I'm afraid of what I'll find on the other side.

I heard the screaming, the fighting. The shattering of glass.

There's no light on in the bathroom, but the stray light streaming in from the hallway reflects off the shards of mirror that litter the floor.

The door only stops when the knob hits the wall, and I stand there frozen in the doorway.

The cuts on his face and hands, the blood that drips down and covers his hand will forever be etched into my memory.

But the sight of him, the man I love so deeply and who I'm desperate to heal all the way down to his very soul, is wretched and it cracks my heart in two.

Sitting on the edge of the tub, his hands cover his face as he's hunched over. But he's alive. Wounded deeply, but still breathing.

"Jay," I whisper his name, terrified I've said the wrong one. I wait with bated breath, the pain in my chest only intensifying as he sits still, ignoring me and making me question what to do.

Call for an ambulance. It's obvious. He needs it. A psychotic break isn't something I can handle on my own.

I take a hesitant step forward, not daring to flick on the light switch. I'm only wearing a pair of socks, but I keep to the right, and gently push the sharp pieces of glass out of my way as I walk toward him. I just need to hold him. I need him to know that it's alright. It doesn't matter how bad it gets, it will always be alright.

The glass clinks as I kick a chunk to the left and take another cautious step toward him.

Finally, he peeks up at me. My body freezes, and I try to figure out if he's there. If Jay is present, or if John is the one sitting in front of me.

I can usually tell by the way he looks at me, but now they both know.

My heart sputters at the pain swirling in his light gray eyes. How his lip twitches with the need to frown and he shakes his head, looking away from me.

"It didn't go well," he speaks just above a murmur and looks away from me, staring at the wall as he lets out a heavy breath. I watch as he tries to relax in front of me, shaking his shoulders and brushing his fingers through

189

his hair. Small pieces of glass tinkle as they drop into the porcelain tub.

Jay.

"You should give me a minute," Jay finally says as he stands tall and towers over me.

"I can help," I offer, but he steps around me, walking to the sink with the glass crunching beneath his boots.

"There's glass," Jay points out the obvious and then stares pointedly at my feet before turning on the faucet.

"I can get shoes," I say weakly. My thoughts are a blur, and his casual demeanor is not at all what I expected. "Can I just clean the glass from your hands so you don't make it worse?" I ask him. My fingers are itching to comfort him. To help him. I'm terrified he'll push me away.

"No," Jay says dismissively, running his hand under the water and looking up to a chunk of mirror still left on the wall. "What happened?" I ask him in a whisper. He looks at me over his shoulder and I think he's going to tell me to just leave, but thankfully he doesn't.

"John doesn't want to believe he did that to you."

I stand there numb, the tips of my fingers tingling. "Did what... did what to me?" I ask. Although I shake my head, there's nothing wrong. "You did nothing wrong."

Jay's lips part and a huff of a humorless laugh leaves him. He dries his hands on the towel, looking straight ahead.

"The day you left is what he's thinking about," he says and his voice is deathly low.

Tears sting at my eyes as I say, "Forgive me." I'll never

190

forgive myself, but please, please I need him to know I regret it with everything in me.

"There's nothing for me to forgive, little bird. You did what I told you to do." He cups my jaw in his strong hand and I lean into his touch, desperate for it. For anything he can give me. "But John hasn't forgiven anything. He hasn't even begun to forgive himself."

I can't imagine the pain. I can't imagine what the man standing right in front of me is feeling in this moment. I just need to be here. And I am, but what good am I?

"I have to clean this up," he says as his hand falls to his side. "Just give me a moment, little bird," he tells me easily and with a small smile I so rarely see. There's a sadness in his eyes too though and I don't understand it. It makes me fear for him. I grab onto his hand, not wanting to leave and not willing to risk him.

"You're scaring me," I tell him honestly.

"I need to clean this."

"I can do it," I offer quickly. Anything I can do to help, but Jay snatches my wrists. The swift motion catches me by surprise. His fingers are forceful and his gaze down at me is intense.

"I need to be alone for a moment," he tells me, but it's the last thing I want for him. He's been alone for so long, and he just needs to let someone help him.

"I just want to help you, Jay." I'm terrified he's close to a break that's simply too much to handle. I can't let that happen. Not to him. Not to someone I love so deeply when I'm right here. "I can help you," I beg him and his expression softens slightly.

He turns my wrist and kisses it gently before letting

me go. "Soon, little bird," he says and his voice is soft and drenched with hopelessness.

"It's going to be okay, Jay," I tell him, feeling the pain in my heart worsen each second that passes without him looking at me.

I follow his gaze to the broken glass and blood on the tiled bathroom floor. I can clean this up. I can fix this. *We* can fix this. "I can get you-"

"Go to your room, little bird," Jay says with authority, cutting me off. My lips part with both disbelief and an objection but he adds, "I love you and I don't want you to see this right now."

I love you. I've known he loves me. How could we not share this together? Two people so deeply intertwined and whose souls who cling to each other for comfort.

My lower lip wobbles and I reach out to him. I grip onto his shoulder without thinking until I'm clinging to his shirt and realize what I've done. But Jay doesn't react, he just lets me pull him and that hurts me deeper than anything. *His fight has waned.*

"I love you. All of you, and I'm right here," I tell him desperately, praying he'll believe me. Every bit of what I've said.

A small trace of a smile forms on his lips and at first I feel like it really will be okay, as if he'll let me help him the way he needs.

"We should go," I offer although my words are shaky and my voice lacking confidence. I don't want him to withdraw.

"I'm not going back," Jay says with a hard voice. He

looks me in the eyes as he tells me, "Go to your room, Robin."

My stomach sinks and churns. He needs help I can't give him. Jay kicks a large piece of glass and I look around. It can wait a moment. Just a moment, but I have to force his hand. This can't happen again.

"I love you, Jay," I tell him with every bit of sincerity in me and reach up on my tiptoes to plant a chaste kiss on the line of his hard jaw before turning to leave.

"I was never Jay," I swear I hear him say as I step into the hallway, but when I turn around, he shuts the door faster than I can move, leaving me alone.

CHAPTER 27

John

Twenty years ago

*T*he ground feels colder today; fall or winter must be coming. It's hard to know without the bit of light from the windows anymore. He took it away.

"Please," she asks me again. She's afraid to ask me for things. At first I thought it was because she was afraid of me. But I think it's something else. A mix of sympathy and guilt. She shouldn't have either toward me. I hate it.

I lean my body so I'm closer to her, but still far enough away not to frighten her. She has a habit of inching closer to me; it's a habit I like. I love it even.

I love that she needs me.

"You don't have to ask, little bird," I say her nickname and she does this cute thing where she smiles and avoids my gaze. It almost makes me smile, but I can't. Not here. This house isn't a place for happiness. I'll smile when I get her out of here. Only then.

"Can you hold my hand, Jay?" she asks me softly, her eyes flickering to mine and then back down to the floor.

I pull the blanket up tighter around her and slip her small hand into mine, weaving our fingers together and letting her hold me like she wants to. She's been calling me Jay since the first day. I should have corrected her, but I don't want her to call me John. I don't want to be John. I don't want this life. I only want to be her Jay.

"I'll always hold your hand," I tell her.

"Always?" she asks, and I merely laugh it off in a huff and tighten my hand around hers. Always is such a long way away. Too long to promise. I know it can't last forever and I won't make a promise I can't keep.

I'll be Jay for her though.

I love her for calling me Jay.

For letting me exist again. Even if it's only for her.

***

THE MEMORY IS SO CLEAR. MY HEAD PULSES AND I TRY TO swallow as I lean against the bathroom counter.

What was I doing here?

Cleaning up the mess you made, a voice, Jay's voice, says so clearly in my head.

I look up to see who it is when the bathroom door opens, letting in the light from the hallway.

"Jay." Robin's voice is quiet, frightened. Jay. My body sways, and a shooting pain in my temple makes me wince. "You need help. I can help you. Please, Jay."

"That's not my name!" I scream at her, feeling light-headed and my lungs refusing to fill. I'm not that sick fuck.

I refuse to believe it. I grip my hair in my hands and try to get the memory out. That never happened to me. I feel sorry for Jay. I can't separate the two.

I close my eyes, trying to figure out what's wrong with me. My head throbs and I can't get these visions to go away. It's because he's told me his past so many times. I close my eyes trying to remember when he told me, but in my memory, he's there, sitting on the chair, leaning against the wall, but then nothing. He's vanished.

"John," Robin says with her hands up. "You need help, John, and it's okay. You're okay, I promise you." She sounds scared and she takes in quick breaths as she speaks, walking toward me slowly.

Like I'm a wounded animal.

Calm for her. I hear Jay's voice and it only makes me angrier. She shouldn't fucking be here.

My vision blurs and for a moment it goes black, but I hold on to the counter. I'm lost right now. I can barely grasp what's real and what's not.

"It's fine," I tell her out of instinct. Because that's what you do when someone's worried for you. You lie to them.

"It's not, John," she says and shakes her head and her small hands wrap around my arm. "You suppressed memories for a reason." Her voice quavers and I wrap my arms around her instantly, hating that she's breaking down. She cries harder and tries to push me away, but I don't let her. I rock her back and forth.

She's so innocent in all of this.

"Just forgive me, please?" she asks me with tears in her eyes.

"For what?" I ask her, not understanding why she's so upset. She hasn't done anything wrong. I'm the one that's so fucked up. I'm the one who hurt her. The one who fucking kidnapped her.

My head spins at the thought. It's all me. Anger boils, but she speaks and I try to calm myself.

"For leaving you behind," she whispers her choked words.

My blood turns to ice as the memories come back again. They keep coming over and over. I try to shut them out but they make a pulsing pain shoot from the back of my head to the front where it stays and throbs, where it punishes me until I acknowledge the past. Until I face what I've done and what I've been through. "It had to happen," I tell her in an even voice, but the anger is there. I can feel it. I hated her for leaving me when I only existed for her. "I was selfish," I whisper as my hands start to shake with the mix of heated emotions.

A small sob leaves her as she shakes her head. "No, you were only a boy," she replies and tries to say something else but I can't hear her over the cries. She wipes her eyes and her shoulders shake.

"It's not your fault, little bird." The words slip out so easily. As if it's natural to call her that. I'm surprised by the presence I feel. As if I'm here holding her. For a moment, my vision splits. I can see me holding her, I can even feel my arm leaning against the wall. It's Jay who's holding her, Jay who recognizes her pain.

But I refuse to do it. I shut my eyes tight and hold her

even tighter. I kiss her hair and a chill runs through my body, followed by a heat that boils my blood.

I may be aware that I am him and vice versa, but that doesn't mean that both sides of me are willing to merge.

"Go to sleep," I tell her in a deep voice. I look her in the eyes as I order her, "Go to your room, Robin."

"Now!" I yell and watch as she obeys me, looking at me with equal amounts of fear and defiance. I lick my lips, not knowing what to do. Everything's changed.

CHAPTER 28

John

"You're not taking this well, are you?" I look up at the sound of Jay's voice. He's standing against the doorframe to the kitchen, staring at me. A phone is in his hand. His phone. I look down at my own hand, and it's there. He tosses it back and forth in his hands, grinning at me and taunting me.

The decision is obvious. I need to call and turn myself in, but I can't fucking bring myself to do it.

I grip the phone tightly before shoving it away from me, but when I look up it's still there, still in *his* hands.

"You're not real," I tell him, refusing to rise and go touch him. Have I ever felt him? I can't remember a time I have. I'm crazy. Legitimately insane.

My mind plays tricks on me. Jay vanishes and my head throbs, memories changing in my head, turning fuzzy then sharp with the truth. The memories coming back.

He smiles, a thin, wicked smile and says, "Of course I am. I'm you."

"Make it stop," I grit from between my teeth, holding my head and rocking back and forth. I stand and scream, "You're not real!"

But who is it that wasn't real? *The life I lived was a lie.* I struggle to breathe as my stomach churns and I realize the very man I pitied, the life I saw as pathetic and disturbing… it was me. *It was mine all along.*

"All those nights I couldn't sleep," I hear Jay say and I look up to search for him, but he's nowhere to be found. I wince as I stumble and grip the wall, my head pounding harder and harder. "All the nights I had to go to her just to know it was real. That it really happened and it haunted her, too."

"Get out of my head!" I scream and seethe with anger. My eyes open slowly and I lift my head, seeing him watching from the corner of the living room.

"And what's worse? I knew I was fucked up in the head. So fucked up I couldn't go to her. I wanted to. So, fucking badly, but because of you, I couldn't!"

Toby barks and snarls, turning to face Jay, to face nothing. His hackles are raised as he exposes his teeth and a vicious growl echoes in the room.

"Jay?" I hear Robin call out from down the hallway, and closest to Jay. Closest to where Toby is facing. To what he sees as a threat.

Not my little bird. My body feels heavy and then light. He's gone and then I'm gone, a blackness taking over. But I fight it. The fur bunches in my hand.

I hear him whine, feel the dog's claws digging into the

ground, and the sounds follow me, although I don't feel present. I'm here but not in control of my actions. Present but weak. Muted by the control Jay has, but conscious of it.

The basement door slams shut, and Toby claws and barks at the door. Over and over, the poor thing trapped but our Robin protected.

Our Robin.

"It's hell, isn't it?" I hear Jay's voice in my head as I come back to what's real. As I struggle to catch my breath and feel the blood from Toby's bite dripping down my arm.

When did he bite me?

"When you grabbed him from behind," I hear Jay say from the other end of the hallway.

"Jay!" Robin calls out from behind the closed door to her room.

"It's a bitch being there but not being present, isn't it?" Jay sneers. "It's fucking hell!" he screams and then stares at Robin's bedroom door.

"I'm coming out," Robin says from behind the door and both of us whip our heads to stare.

"Stay inside!" he screams before I can, but the words come from me, I can feel it. My body, but not my mind.

I don't want her out here, I think but don't say.

She's not a part of this, I hear in my own head. I look up and he's gone.

"You brought her here," I say out loud with spite.

"I can help, we need to talk," Robin says and her words are muted by the closed door.

"How could you bring her here?" I ask him as my body trembles. My poor Robin. She can't be here.

"You slept. Well you thought you slept, with not a fucking worry in the world. All the while, all I am is a fucking ghost of what happened to us! You kept me back to feel better," he spits the last two words.

"Selfish fuck!" I spit the words as the bedroom door opens. In two large strides I'm at the door and pulling the handle hard so it shuts.

"Stay inside!" I scream at her while Jay fights for control, or does he? I don't know anymore. My head pulses again with pain.

"I'm not going away, John."

I grab both sides of my head, falling against the hallway.

"Jay, please," I hear Robin call as the door creaks open again.

"Get out," I tell him as my hands ball into tight fists. They pound my head time and again.

"Please let me help you." She's cautious and doesn't move from her spot, but she opens the door slowly.

"You do this to me!" Jay's voice forces my eyes up to the corner of the hallway as Robin approaches me. He screams back at me, his eyes glossy and suddenly I see him for who he really is. "This is who you are!"

"Jay, please," Robin says and walks toward me with her hands up. She's walking into the fire.

She's not safe.

"Get out," I tell her as I press my hand to the wall and steady myself. "Get out of here," I bite out the words as she flinches and takes a half step back.

"I'm not leaving you," she says quietly beneath her breath, her eyes wide with both fear and disbelief. Jay's voice echoes in my head as he screams, but I don't listen.

"Get out," I say calmly, all the rage just beneath the surface. She tries to turn, to run back to her room, but I'm faster than her. I close the door and slam it shut before she can run. I cage her small body in, loving the heat and the feel.

I fucking love her, and that makes the pain in my chest only splinter deeper.

"Get out," I repeat again, feeling her hair in my face and resisting the urge to touch her, to comfort her as she trembles beneath me.

"I can help," she barely gets out as she turns in the small space between us.

"That's why I'm here," she pleads with me, chancing a moment to reach out to me. Her small hands reach up to my chest and I feel Jay inside of me. I feel him cower in pain and agony.

I'm a monster. "He never should have brought you here," I tell her and grab her wrists.

Her breath shudders as I tug her away.

"No!" she yells as she kicks me and runs to the living room.

I grind my teeth and follow her in, right on her heels. She grabs onto the first thing she sees, the sofa, and grips it as if it will protect her.

"John, no," she pleads with me, but she doesn't turn.

My breath stills and I feel Jay pace inside, hating me and wanting to kill me as I pry her fingers from the edge of the sofa.

She can't stay. I won't let her see this.

Jay's quiet as I fight her, holding her small body against mine and force her from the house. She kicks and begs me over and over, but I ignore her.

As I toss her outside, careful to keep her from falling too much, I know how this needs to end.

CHAPTER 29

Robin

*F*ear laces my blood and the night air is bitter cold, making my hands shake as I reach into my pocket for his phone I took from him as he forced me out. I'm glad I had the presence of mind to put on my shoes when I went back to my room. I did it to avoid being cut by the broken glass in the bathroom but I should have realized this would be a possibility as well.

My shoes slam down on the porch steps, one after the other as I run forward. I look behind me, over my shoulder, breathing heavily from the terror screaming in my blood.

I knew there was a chance he'd break. Every moment with John I waited for him to remember. It fucking killed me for him to look at me with new eyes. No memory of everything we'd gone through. It was selfish of me, but I needed to know if he'd still love me even if I kept the truth at bay. That selfish desire stayed my hand. That, and the fear of how he'd handle it once he learned the truth.

Once he's learned who he truly is.

My Jay. The tortured boy and my savior in every way. But he doesn't see it as that. He never could.

My shoulder brushes against the bark of a tree as I try to catch my breath, breathing in the cold night air that makes my lungs feel like they've frozen. My muscles scream from running as fast as I did, but this is as far as I'll go.

I lean my body against the thick oak tree and look back at the house. The sounds of him yell, pull more pain from my heart. The sob is suppressed as the light from the phone brightens the dark night and tears my eyes away from the lit windows in John's house.

There's no one for miles. No help can come soon enough.

There's no fucking way I'm leaving him. He's a danger to himself.

I stare at the screen, looking at the numbers to press to unlock it.

A password.

Fuck! I chew the inside of my cheek, looking back up at the house. I don't know his fucking number! In a moment of panic, I almost forget that there's an emergency call option at the bottom. I silence the sob that tears its way out from my lips and quickly call the police.

I clench my teeth. No rings. Pick up. Pick up!

A loud bang, like a crash from inside the house makes my heart leap in my chest and my body turns to ice as I look up. Nothing to see, nothing to hear but Toby's barking, over and over.

The click is loud as a calm female voice speaks clearly, "Emergency operator, what-"

"I need help!" I scream into the phone.

"What's your address, ma'am?" the woman asks me, and I freeze. Fuck! I look around, I look everywhere for a mailbox or a number. There's only a dirt road.

"I don't know! I don't know!" I scream into the phone, tears stinging my eyes. I look up at the house again, feeling like I'm failing him. "I don't know," I croak and cover my mouth, hating how weak I sound.

"Is the emergency at the location of your phone?" the woman asks me and I nod my head as I answer her, "Yes, please come fast."

"I've got your address. The police are on their way. I need to know what-"

As soon as she tells me they're coming, I drop the phone and bolt to the house. Finally help is coming for him. *Finally*.

"Jay!" I cry out as I grip the wooden railing and race up the stairs. The screen door slams open as I rush to get inside. As soon as I enter the house, I hear Toby barking again.

But it turns to white noise. Nothing matters as I sway on numb legs and stare at the ground.

The bookshelf is splintered on the ground, the books are strewn about. The lamp is shattered, and covering the floor with shards of thin glass are specks of blood that get larger and larger as I walk quietly to the other side of the room.

"Jay?" I call out, just as my eyes lock on his limp body in the middle of the room. The coffee table is overturned and he's lying next to it. Where he lay the first night I snuck from my room to see him.

"John?" I call out his name out of desperation. I walk faster when there's no response, falling to my knees next to him. His face is bloodied and bruised, as are his knuckles. A large mark on his face is bright red, covering nearly half of it and it's then that I realize he slammed his head repeatedly into the coffee table.

I put my hand on his chest, shaking him gently. "Talk to me, please," I whimper, but he's still. "Say something!"

I press my fingers to the side of his wrist, but fail to find a pulse. I press harder out of sheer panic. There's nothing. "Jay!" I scream a strangled cry and wrap my fingers around his wrist, holding his hand with mine.

"How could you?" I whisper. He can't leave me. "You can't leave me," I barely get out. "I love you. I love all of you and I can help you," I tell him in a ragged voice through the sobs.

Regret and fear are consuming me. *He can't die.*

It's only when I put my fingers beneath his nose and feel his breath that I'm somewhat calmed. But his pulse is so weak. "Help me!" I scream, knowing no one can hear. The tears fall down my cheeks freely, my eyes already are swollen and stinging from the pain.

I can't breathe as I hold his head in my lap, the warmth of the blood soaking through my clothes.

My body rocks back and forth. "Stay with me, Jay, please."

"John, come back to me."

"I love you both. I promise I'll make it better. I swear I'll never leave you again." As I whisper the promise I faintly hear sirens making their way toward the house. Help is coming. Finally, help is coming for him. I sniffle and hold him closer, lowering my head and whispering next to his ear, "I'm so sorry." I can't even voice everything I regret.

The sounds of the sirens coming can be heard in the distance, getting closer now.

"Just please come back to me."

CHAPTER 30

John

*B*eep. *Beep. Beep.*

Each time the machine sounds, my head throbs with a pain that only brings back memories. I feel my forehead pinch and another shooting pulse, but I can't move my hand up to my head.

I groan, trying to move but I can't.

The images flash through my head.

My father holding me down. *Beep.*

His fist. *Beep.*

The dogs. *Beep.*

I go backward in time.

My mother dying. *Beep.*

I want to stay there. They're so happy. He holds her, and she holds me. *Beep.*

She's on the ground. *Beep.*

She won't wake up. *Beep.*

I scream out for her.

My head shakes and I try to move again, feeling closer to consciousness, becoming more aware of my body, but it's so heavy.

I shake her shoulders, trying to get her to wake up. Mom! I scream out. Mom!

The sound of my father's boots. The sound of the toolbox that crashes to the ground as he runs into the room.

My throat feels raw as I cry out again. *Beep.*

He pushes me out of the way.

No! Mom! *Beep.*

My shoulders shake as I watch him leaning over her.

Small hands shake me, but they aren't in the room with me.

Father! Help her! *Beep.*

His cold gaze finds me, his hands still holding Mom, but when he looks back at me, I can't cry out anymore. I can't speak.

His eyes are like ice as he sneers at me. What did I do? Why is he blaming me? I didn't do anything. I swear I didn't.

"Jay!" I hear a voice scream, and my eyes part slowly. My groggy head sways and I try to blink. The bright lights hurt though. My wrists sting as I pull upward, but they won't move. It takes a moment as my head lolls to the side to realize I'm in the hospital. Sedated and restrained.

"Jay," I hear her soft voice and vaguely feel her hands on mine. I turn my hand slightly and she laces her small fingers with mine. *My little bird.* I've held her hand so many times. Her hand belongs in mine. Everything's okay then. That's all I need to know that everything's okay.

Robin, my little bird.

She brought me here.

I expect anger, I expect to hate her. Instead I only feel weak and helpless. The pain in her voice is what does it. I've hurt her. I'll do anything, my little bird. Don't leave me. Not here, and not ever.

Slowly, the memories come back.

All twenty years and more.

My Robin. My sweet Robin.

I watch her run. I keep watching as the dogs bark behind me. They're so close, and I'm certain they're going to get out. It's only a large stick keeping the cage secured. It's going to break. I know it will. But when it does, they'll come for me.

I'll watch her though. I'll make sure up until the last moment my life slips from me that she's free, that she's running and the dogs stay here. My father will stay here. They can have me, so long as she's free.

When I turn behind me, finally ripping my eyes away from where she's gone, it's only because the sound of boots stomping against the cold hard ground is getting louder. It's only because I don't want him to touch me. But the second I turn, the shovel slams against my skull and blackness consumes me. Only the briefest vision of my father follows me to the darkness.

"Jay, please. Stay with me," I hear her soft voice call out. It's like an echo in my head.

I'm here. I try to tell her, but my throat isn't working. My voice isn't here. I'm here, little bird. We made it. We both made it.

I remember standing outside her house. Across the

street and shielded from the row of oak trees, I waited for her to be alone. She came to mine and I followed her home, too afraid of the police. I did that. I burned it down. It was all my fault.

But she has a family who holds her so closely.

And she never looked back.

My hand slips from the tree and the rough bark scrapes my arm. When she ran away... she never looked back. As the anger rises, I hear the footsteps behind me. I turn ready to fight, my movements sharp.

But there's no one there. Just a voice in my head. I shake my head again. The boy is there. He looks the way I want to look. Who am I?

"Jay!" Robin's voice is clear and strong.

"Robin," I finally answer her and I know she heard it.

Beep. "Turn off," I try to speak but my throat hurts too much.

"You were intubated, Jay. It's okay," I hear her tell me as I fight against the bindings holding me down.

I open my eyes as she yells at someone to turn off the machine.

They tied me up. I stare at the bindings, hating her. She of all people should know.

"Jay, it's okay," she tells me as she pats my hand over my clenched fist. "You had ICU psychosis and you tried to rip out your IVs, but you're okay." Her words barely register as I pull at the bindings, my muscles coiled, but I'm weak.

"Please, Jay. Please stop," Robin begs me, her voice

strained. Her small hands grab my face, and they're so soft. Her tears hit my chest hard.

It's only then I see the wires, all the machines.

"Miss," a nurse calls out behind Robin as she comes forward to take my Robin away.

"Leave me alone!" Robin cries out and then looks back at me, her hazel eyes pleading with me. "Stay with me, Jay. Please. It's been days of this. Please, Jay. Stay with me."

Days?

I still my body, my heart beating rapidly and thumping so hard in my chest it hurts.

"He's fine!" I hear Robin snap at someone behind her and then sniffle. "Don't put him back under. He'll be okay. I know he will," she says and her voice is so strong.

"Robin, what-?" I can't finish my sentence as the last memory comes to the forefront of my mind. Over and over I smashed my head against the wall and coffee table, against anything. I wanted him out of my head. Jay... the memories of Jay.

I swallow thickly as Robin talks quietly and calmly, in an even cadence meant to avoid agitation.

"You hurt yourself," she tells me. "You're okay now, but I need to make sure you can swallow on your own and eat."

"Swallow?" I ask her.

"When you first came in, you woke up and... and they had to sedate you, Jay." Her small hand grips my arm tight. She's so sad as she tells me what's happened.

"Do they know?" I ask her and then swallow, my throat throbbing from the pain. I don't care if they hear. I need help. I can't hurt my Robin. I won't do it.

I see her nod in my periphery and it draws my attention to her. I try to pull my arm up so I can brush her tears away, but I can't and I've never felt a greater pain in my life.

"It's called Dissociative Identity Disorder... or split personality as it's more commonly called."

I nod once, I know already. I've known all along, but part of me has held it down. There is no cure. There are times when you may forget again and slip into psychosis, but constant therapy and a desire to be well are important. I used to think it was because my dad was crazy. It's not genetic. But it can arise from abuse and stress.

"Could you undo these please?" Robin's voice comes out strained as she angrily wipes under her eyes. "He's fine now," she says confidently. "He's back," she whispers.

I can't look as a nurse unties the bindings and tells me something. Not to hit, not to harm myself. It all turns to a blur as I think about her staying with me for days.

"How many days?" I ask her, although I stare straight ahead at the white wall.

"It's been six days," she says and I close my eyes tight. As the binding to my left wrist loosens, I quickly move it to my right, on top of Robin's.

"You stayed with me?" I ask her and she nods her head but says, "They couldn't let me stay with you at night at first. I had to get papers and orders."

It's quiet for a long time. And I whisper, "I'm sorry." I truly am. For everything I've put her through. She doesn't answer me, she only kisses my cheeks and then once chastely on my lips, but I can't open my eyes.

"Your name is John?" Robin asks me.

My voice is raspy as I answer her, "Yes."

I lay my head back, remembering how she ran again. How I gave her a choice and she left, but yet she's here.

I speak from the heart. Without thinking at all I say, "You don't owe me anything, Robin. I knew you'd run, and I knew I'd have to stay behind. You never owed me anything. You never had anything to be sorry for, Robin. This guilt isn't on you." I know she needs to hear it. It's plagued her for so long. My eyes stay closed, and I can't bear to look at her to see her reaction. I need to let her go for good.

"Stop it, John," I hear her say and turn my head to her.

"You aren't mine to keep," I tell her as my gaze finds hers. I want to keep her though. So badly.

"I was always yours, Jay." A warmth floods my chest, until I hear the name.

"Jay," I say the name with anger. I hid behind Jay. Or maybe I hid behind both. I don't even know which is more present in this moment.

"You've always been Jay to me. Always. And I've always loved you."

"I don't deserve you," I tell her simply.

"It's not about what we deserve, only about what's real."

"What's real?" I repeat her words with a sarcastic laugh. "My name's John." I talk out loud, but not really talking to Robin, my sweet little bird. Just at the mere thought of her nickname, the sight of her looking up from the floor of my father's cellar to the small dirty window flashes into my mind.

"You'll be alright, I promise you," she reassures me

then cups my chin and kisses me on the lips. I grip her wrists, wanting to push her away. I don't deserve her love, and she shouldn't have to deal with this. With how fucked up I am.

"Hey," she whispers and tilts my chin slightly so I look her in her eyes. "Now that you know, now that you're aware, it will be much easier. I promise you." She licks her lips and stares deep into my eyes, willing me to believe her. "I know everything's going to be okay. It will take time, but just you knowing and accepting… you have no idea how difficult that is."

"It's because of you," I tell her. "He used you to make me-" I clear my throat and correct myself. "I used you," I confess and my heart splinters just admitting it. I can feel the urge to hold her tighter making my hands itch. The memories of my father coming on strong and making me want to cling to her. Everything was better when she was there.

"You did what you had to do," she tells me, but there's no way she can convince me that it's justified.

"I don't care what you think or where we came from," she says. "John, Jay, it's just a name. I love you. I've loved you for years. All I need to know is whether or not you love me."

Of course I do. She's the only one I've ever loved. I don't even know if it's possible to love someone else like I love her. She rests her hand against my cheek and my eyes drift to hers. "Do you love me?" she asks me in a whisper of a breath. The fear and insecurity apparent.

I tell her the truth. What I know to be more real than anything else. "I've always loved you, Robin. When I was jealous, when I hated what you represented, when I feared what you could do to me and what power you held over me." A sob rips from her throat and she covers her mouth with both of her hands as tears leak down her cheeks. I brush them away and put my hand on the nape of her neck, gently but firmly, just how she is with me. With a small push, she falls closer to me and I rest my forehead against hers and lower my hand to her back to rub soothing strokes up and down. "I've always loved you, Robin. And I always will."

CHAPTER 31

Robin

Two weeks have gone by, and sometimes John forgets. It's remarkable that he was able to live a relatively normal life before. But I don't want him to have anything but a full life from this day onward.

I'll never leave him again. And he knows better than to pull that shit again.

The paper crinkles in my hand as I set it back down and then carefully fold it to put it back in the envelope. It's the report on John's mother's death. Margaret. He wanted to know, and I'm doing everything I can to find out every little piece of his history. An overdose.

The memories he has of his mother are pleasant, but the detailed history of her past isn't. I don't know how he'll take it, but it's one more piece of information he can digest.

I hear the tea kettle whistle in the kitchen and it rouses me from my seat at the dining room table. As I make my way in, I nearly stumble over the stack of empty cardboard boxes.

Thank fuck I still have a few more weeks left of sabbatical leave. Moving is a nightmare and a half. The kettle silences as I pull it off the stove and instantly hear the rumble of John's truck.

It's odd that the most unbelievable thing to me is that Jay's name was always and has always been John. I'm the only one to have ever called him Jay. A part of me loves it, and a part of me hates it.

The front door opens as I pour the water into the cup. I watch as the steam rises and the bit of calm normalcy is enough to make me smile as I hear his boots smacking on the hardwood floor.

I dunk the tea bag in and then again, watching as the light brown water turns darker and the color consumes the inside of the white ceramic tea cup.

My eyes lift at the sound of John picking up the boxes in the living room. The cardboard rustles as he lets out a heavy sigh.

"Why is there so much yellow?" he asks me. The question makes me smile into the cup and I nod my head once, recognizing the odd obsession.

"Yellow makes you happy," I say simply. "Just seeing the color makes you happier than you were before." I smile at him, but there's a sadness in his eyes from the admission.

He may think he's the fucked up one, but I needed him too. Desperately.

"Is this the last of it?" John asks and then leans against the doorway to the kitchen, ignoring my answer. His white shirt has a bit of dust swiped across the bottom which only makes him appear that much more masculine. His muscles flex under the thin fabric, pulled tightly across his broad shoulders and I absently blow across the top of the mug as I nod my head yes.

Slowly, we're making this place ours. A complete home. It's funny how even our décor seems to need each other for balance.

"Thank you for bringing it all," I tell him. I almost say Jay, but instead I say nothing.

It's odd calling him John, because he's always been Jay to me. He never told me, but I can understand why. In a lot of ways, we're learning more about each other, but in other ways, we're learning who we are ourselves.

Love isn't something we have to learn though. Love was a given from the moment we saw each other. Something in our very souls told us we were meant to be together. Without each other, we wouldn't have survived what life had planned for us. Not back then when we were only children, and not today or even tomorrow.

I need him as much as he needs me. It's the only thing I'm certain of.

"Thank you for staying with me," he says easily as he walks across the kitchen and wraps his arms around my waist. I set the cup down on the counter and the ceramic clinks before I look back up to him. I notice how his hands tighten on me as I lift my hands to his shoulders and rise up on my tiptoes to kiss him on the lips. It's short and chaste, but I want all the kisses from him. Every sort he has for me.

When I pull away and my heels hit the floor, his eyes

are still closed. It's the raw emotion and truth that drew him to me. And maybe me to him.

"Tell me what you remember?" he asks me in a whisper and my gaze falls, but I rest my cheek to his chest and nod my head, listening to the steady sound of his heartbeat.

Together we'll get through it all. Together and always.

"I think you loved me when you saw me, didn't you?" I ask him.

"Which side of me are you asking?" he lets out an uneasy sigh, avoiding my gaze and the question.

"Both, neither, it doesn't matter really. I already know you did," I speak with feigned confidence. I want to hear him say it. I need to, really. I need to know that he's always felt this way. I know I have. I'll never stop loving him and I'm terrified that one day, he'll stop loving me.

"He showed me a picture," he starts to say and then covers his face with his hands. "I... I," John says. I bite my lip, hating how much pain it causes him when he tries to recall a memory and he reverts. But it's normal. He has to learn that. He has to accept it.

"When I saw you, all those years ago, I knew I was to protect you. When I looked at your picture. When I knew I was going to take you and face this... this hell in order to be with you. I looked at your picture and I knew I was going to love you." He nods his head, closing his eyes and I know it hurts, to merge the memories and meld the scene in his head. The medication helps the present, but the past is hard. Nothing's going to change that.

"I love every part of you, the man who wants to forget and the man who suffered for his father's sins." I cup his face in my hand and kiss him on his jaw and then softly on his lips.

He stares back at me with nothing but pain in his eyes.

"I don't know how you can love me," he says in a whisper.

"I don't know how you can think I ever didn't love you. Even when I ran. I've always loved you." A weak smile forces its way to my face as I struggle to use his name. He doesn't want me to call him Jay, but he's always been Jay to me. "My wolf."

John stares back at me, confused for a moment. Sometimes it's like this, when he doesn't quite remember, but then it clicks.

"Wolf," he huffs a sarcastic laugh and shakes his head. "You don't need a wolf, little bird. You needed another, someone just like you. You needed Jay."

I nod my head as my heart splinters. "I need *all* of you," I whisper against his lips. I can feel it, the moment Jay comes to the surface, the moment the possessive man inside of him moves his hands to the back of my head and deepens the kiss.

I pull back and look into his eyes whispering, "Jay?"

A small smile tugs his lips up, only just and he says quietly, "You can call me whichever name you'd like." He rests his forehead against mine and it's then that I realize our past needs to stay where it belongs. "You can call me Jay if you want. I'll be anyone for you. I'll do anything for you. I only exist for you."

I brush my nose against his, trying to lighten the mood. "Maybe when I'm mad at you I'll call you Jay," I tease and try to smile and when he does, my lips turn up easily.

"I love you, John," I tell him quietly, brushing my fingers against his lips. "And I love Jay, too. Both sides of you."

"I love you, little bird." He says the words just like he always has, with a hint of teasing and a touch of darkness.

I lean against him, and he holds me tightly. I wouldn't have it any other way. We're both broken from what happened to us. But the love that's come from it can't tear us apart. As long as we stay together.

"Always?" I ask him.

"Always."

***

JOHN

I CAN HEAR THE SHOWER RUNNING AS I STOP IN FRONT OF the shower door. The tips of my fingers tap against the wood. She's waiting for me, and so many times I think I should leave her. As if I'm undeserving of her and hurting her, keeping her back.

I close my eyes and let out a slow breath. When I inhale, the gentle smell of lavender fills my lungs. It's what my little bird smells like. And just that little bit makes the memories of holding her come back to me. They flood to me now. The bad ones I try to ignore, but the ones with her, *the ones with my little bird,* I hold on to them with everything I have.

It's why I want to let her go. And why I never will.

My eyes pop open wide, the selfishness and depravity making me hate the thought. She's a grown woman though, and she knows who I am in every sense of the word. As long as she wants me, I'm staying with her.

I push the door open slowly and the steam greets me with warmth and slowly passes behind me.

The anger surprises me sometimes, but more than that, the fear.

My father's dead and burned to ashes, but the fear is very much alive. I always knew the other side of me was filled with a darkness, but I wouldn't have thought it was fear.

But that's what creeps up more than anything. Especially at night.

Until my wife leans against me, giving me much-needed warmth. Until my hand splays across her belly and we both fall easily to sleep.

"I heard something about you always being right," I tease and then pull the shirt over my head. She peeks out from the shower curtain with a quip on her lips, something smart no doubt, but instead her eyes fall to my chest and the thought is long gone.

A deep groan of satisfaction rumbles up my chest and her eyes reach mine as a blush creeps up her chest and she pulls the curtain back into place to hide behind.

I fucking love it. I love her. And to think, I may have never had her.

The past can ruin a person forever. They may recover,

but they're never the same. Never what they once were. The scar may be thicker than delicate skin. It may protect you from some things and give you a wall to hide behind.

But it's the gentle things that will cut it open and leave you raw and wounded once again.

Love is gentle and unassuming. It won't be denied.

My love saved me in so many ways, my little bird.

I could forget the pain and burdens.

I could forget the fear that the monster would return. Or worse, that I would be like him.

I could forget it all and leave it where it belongs, in the past.

But I can't forget Robin or the genuine love I felt for her. I can't deny that.

Not when I'm so desperate for her.

Not when she needs me in return.

And not when she's right here, loving me with everything she has and only wanting the same in return.

My memory destroyed me, but love is so much more.

You can't forget love, no matter how hard you try.

EPILOGUE

Robin
Two years later

"Toby!" I call as the dog runs from the porch and out into the field. He looks over his shoulder and halts in his path, but I wave him off. He can run if he wants to.

I sway easily on the porch swing, the chatter from inside muted by the screen door and the faint hum of the water flowing from the creek out back. I love it out here, on this property and in this house that John built.

Two years we've been here. Making steady progress. It may not always be perfect, but we're safe with each other. And John hasn't forgotten me and he believes what I tell him about our past. He remembers somethings too which makes days hard here and there, but together we'll pull through. That's the most important part. The trust and love between us are strong enough to keep us together.

Just as my eyes drift shut, the screen door opens with a

long groan. I pop them open quickly, pretending like the exhaustion isn't getting to me.

"You coming back in?" John asks me. He's got a smile on his face and I know he loves this. "After all, the celebration is all for you," he says and his eyes drift to my swollen belly.

"It's not for me," I say with my eyes closed as the little one kicks my hip again. My feet slip across the porch floor as I shift on the swing and try to get more comfortable.

John lets the screen door shut and crosses the porch to sit with me. The swing dips when he sits and wraps his arm around me to pull me closer to him.

"They're here for you," John whispers into my ear and splays his hand over my belly. I love it when he does that. When his eyes light up with hope. We didn't plan this little one, but I'm so grateful and happy. And so is John.

I kiss him, feeling a rush of warmth flow through me. I would never have guessed our lives would turn out like this. It's nearly picture perfect.

At the sound of the door opening again, I pull away, feeling the heat of a blush on my cheeks. John just smiles as he stands and helps me to my feet. The wooden swing gently hits the back of my legs as I get my balance and say goodbye to a group of my coworkers.

"We're heading out," Karen says as she waves her hand, the other occupied by a paper plate covered with aluminum foil. A young woman who must be in her early forties, or maybe late thirties walks out with the group. She's in her gardening clothes and in an instant, I know she's one of our new neighbors. They live down the road and closer to John's shop. The closest neighbors we have.

"I really appreciate the invitation," she says as she stops in front of us. I've only had a few conversations with her, but she's a sweet woman, alone out here for the most part.

"Of course," I answer her. "I'm so happy you came." I can't help the smile on my face or the small yawn that comes after it as John makes small talk with her. I watch him as he talks. It's night and day from where he was just two short years ago. He's not perfect, but neither am I. Together though, we've gotten through everything. One thing that the memory can always hold on to, is love. There's never a doubt in either of us that the other person doesn't truly love them. That's rare and special and I can't get over how powerful it is.

"How did you two meet?" our new neighbor asks as she grips her drink in both of her hands. She looks between the two of us with a smile on her face. "You're such a good-looking couple," she says. I wish the smile that wants to come to the surface were genuine, but it's not.

She's not the first to ask.

And a part of me deep down is terrified that they'll all find out the truth. Another part wants to scream it out loud and tell everyone what we've gone through. Together.

I keep the smile on my face as my husband wraps his arm around my shoulder and pulls me closer to him. A lie slips so easily from his lips. It's a struggle every time, to listen to words that are false, meant to hide the truth.

No one wants to hear our story. The *real* story. When

they ask how we met, no one would expect the harsh reality of our pasts. No one would be able to understand. They would judge us. And they'd never forget it.

I sure as fuck won't.

It's dark and twisted.

But that doesn't make it any less of what it is.

A love story. *Our* love story.

AND I'M SO GRATEFUL WE GOT A HAPPILY EVER AFTER. Stories like ours aren't meant to end like this. It's only because we stayed together. Only because our love was stronger than our pain.

The End

Don't stop reading! Looking for another dark romance? Try Broken! Keep reading for a sneak peek!

Sign up for Text Alerts:
US residents: Text WILLOW to 797979
UK residents: Text WWINTERS to 82228

And if you're on Facebook, join my reader group, Willow Winters' Wildflowers for special updates and lots of fun!

SNEAK PEEK AT BROKEN

From *USA Today* bestselling author W Winters comes an emotionally gripping, standalone, romantic suspense with an edge of darkness.

I never thought of life like the petals of a rose before.
   But they're so alike.
   Delicate and easily crushed.

Broken… just like he made me.
   He could pluck away and there was nothing I could do except be destroyed and accept my fate.

That's what he does, he ruins what he touches. Ruthless and cold hearted.

They gave me to him.

To break.

To do as he'd like.

All because I was in the wrong place at the wrong time.

He grew addicted to the feel of plucking away at me. At leaving me bare and taking control over every piece of me.

And if I'm honest with myself... I grew to love it too.

PROLOGUE

Olivia

$\mathcal{T}$he courtroom is quiet. I can hear someone in the back of the room clear their throat. I swallow thickly and try to avoid their gazes. But I'm on the witness stand, I can't avoid them or any of this.

They're all watching me. Waiting for an answer. I feel like I'm suffocating. This is too much.

It reminds me of being in the room with him. With Kade. My eyes dart to him, and my mouth parts slightly as I remember the time I spent with him.

The other men would watch. He said I had to be perfect, and if I was he'd give me my freedom. And he did. He's a man of his word. But this freedom feels empty and hollow. I wish I could take it back. Not our time together, just my wish to be set free.

"Miss Bell?" asks the prosecution, snapping me out of my reverie.

"Yes?" I ask warily. My fingers twist in my hand. My heartbeat picks up. I don't want to be here. I'd give anything to go back.

They're waiting for me to talk, to testify against him and give evidence that Kade's a bad man. That he deserves to be imprisoned not only for what he did to me, but for everything else.

But I can't. He did it to protect me. He *had* to do it. My voice is caught in my throat. My blood heats and chills at the same time. The thought of turning against him makes me sick.

My eyes focus on him, and all I want to do is to run to his side. I wish he could just take me away. Instead he's on trial, and I'm left alone to deal with the aftermath of how my life has changed forever.

Tears prick my eyes as Kade nods his head and gives me a small, sad smile. He wants me to answer them. He wants me to be a good girl and tell them everything they want to know so I can go free. *It's time to let go, angel.* I hear his words and I hate them. I don't want to let go of him. I was his, and now I feel like I'm no one.

"Do you need me to repeat the question?" the old man says as he stares at me through his spectacles.

I shake my head. I know what he asked. I know what they want from me.

My body relaxes as I remember how he broke me down bit by bit. Now it seems calculated, as though he knew what he was doing. Like he used me. That's what they keep telling me, they say that's why I feel this way about him. But back then, it felt different. It felt as though he was helping me. I thought he needed me. *He did need me.*

His fingers gently slid down the curve of my hip. *"My angel,"* he whispered. His lips barely touched the shell of my ear, his hot breath sending chills down my shoulder. As his hand slid farther down, he groaned with satisfaction. I was always ready for him. I learned to love what he did. I learned to be perfect for him.

"Miss Bell, answer the question." The judge's voice rings out and makes my body jolt in the seat.

I clear my throat thinking about where I should start and what all I should tell them. My heart clenches in my chest. I don't want to share it with them. Right now these memories are mine. They'll ruin them. They'll make me think my recollections are something they aren't.

They want me to believe he never loved me, and that the feelings I have for him are false.

I don't know what to do. I don't know what to believe.

The only thing I know that's true is I fell in love with Kade and that now, because of him, I'm utterly and completely broken.

OLIVIA

THREE MONTHS EARLIER...

I feel sick to my stomach. I wish I could just throw up and be done with this feeling, but it's not from drinking too much, or food poisoning, or anything like that. I'm just sick of my life and the shitty position I put myself in.

Getting turned down for your ninth job interview sucks. And it was for a hair salon. Like, really? All I'd be doing is bookwork. It can't be that fucking hard. I'm starting to think there's no hope. That's what makes me so damn sick. Like there's nothing I can do, and I'm just screwed.

It's been three weeks since I got expelled from the university. It was all over alcohol. They have a zero tolerance policy. So of course getting kicked out also meant losing my scholarships. And losing my scholarships meant losing my income, plus my part-time job in the registrar's office. Which means when the rent is due, I'm fucked if I can't hurry up and land a job already.

As if this wasn't already the worst month of my life,

my mother won't even answer my calls. It's her idea of tough love. Yeah, I know I fucked up. I don't need to hear it again. It's not like this is what I usually do. Like I went to college and suddenly became a horrible person. I was in all the honors classes in high school. I was a teacher's pet.

I've gotten straight A's my entire life, except for that one C in Advanced Literature. Fuck English, I only took the class because I had to in order to fulfill my graduation requirements.

I've always been a brown-noser, as Cheryl calls me.

Fuck, Cheryl. It's her fault!

I bite my lip and cross my arms over my chest to warm myself up. I shake my head, trying not to be bitter about it all. It's not really Cheryl's fault. She may have put the bottle in my hand, but she didn't make me drink. She was only trying to help. After all, it's not every day that your first real boyfriend, the man you gave your virginity to, dumps you for someone prettier.

Tears prick my eyes, but I'm sure as shit not going to cry over him. I'll cry over my self-esteem though, because that shit hurt. When I asked him how he could just break up with me like our relationship meant nothing to him, he just shrugged and said her tits were bigger. Fucking asshole. How did I ever fall for him?

Daniel Croast is hot and athletic, and really knows how to lay on the charm.

But he's a fucking dick. I knew this, yet I still fell for him. I still spread my legs for him and let him take every last piece of me that he wanted.

Curse my fucking hormones. Tall, with broad shoulders. He played on the rugby team and there's just something about men crashing into each other and taking those brutal hits; it makes my pussy pulse with desire. I'm not a biology major, but it was definitely my fucked-up hormones.

I fell in lust, not love.

I finally had a boyfriend and friends. Real friends who liked me for me. Cheryl may be a bad influence and not have a clue about how the real world works, but deep down I know she cares about me.

Drinking on campus in the dorms was stupid though.

Real fucking stupid. I just went there to cry to Audrey about everything, and instead we ended up drinking. I even thought, *No, we should go to our apartment if we're going to be drinking.* Shit, that's the entire reason we got the apartment off-campus.

But I felt horrible, and my friends were all around me, and I just wanted to feel better.

I fucking hate that RA prick that busted us. I swear he's got a stick shoved up his ass. He can go to hell for all I care.

I turn twenty-one in two months, and Cheryl in three. That RA's so fucking pretentious and likes to pretend he did this for the "right reasons" but seriously, he can go fuck himself. He's never liked Audrey since she turned his scrawny ass down during freshman orientation. That's really what it was about, his dumb fucking vendetta.

Luckily for Audrey, she left to go get more booze. And while she was walking to the liquor store, campus security showed up. She got a strike, and we got booted.

So now I'm at the lowest point in my life.

What kills me the most is that my parents aren't talking to me, which I don't understand. I know they're disappointed and all, but the silent treatment is just not helpful. All it's doing is hurting me. I stop at the edge of the sidewalk and wait, standing in the chill of the fall night, hugging my arms tighter around myself. My legs are freezing since I wore a black A-line skirt to my interview, but at least I grabbed my cream chenille sweater.

I stare up at the red hand on the crosswalk sign and just wait.

There aren't any cars this late at night. But the hand is red. And that means you can't go, so I don't. I'm not a fan of breaking the rules.

I huff a laugh at this train of thought. The one time in my entire life I break the rules, and of course I get caught. And now everything I've worked so damn hard for is crumbling all around me. Tears prick at my eyes again, and this time one escapes.

I breathe out slow and steady, calming myself. I wipe the stray tear with the cuff of my sweater and start walking as soon as I get the green signal to go. Mascara covers the end of my sleeve now, but I don't care.

I feel like I'm balanced on the edge of a razor. On one side, I care entirely too much about everything, and my heart aches with all the disappointment I've caused, not to mention the disappointment I feel in myself. But on the other side, I don't give a fuck about any of this. I've hardened my heart with hate for everyone around me that doesn't care enough to try to help.

I swallow thickly. They don't have to help me. No one owes me anything, and that's just fine by me. I have a plan.

This isn't going to ruin me.

Yes, I got kicked out of one of the most prestigious universities in the country, but I can get into another. If I can just get a job, I can survive until February for sure. That's when I'll find out if I got in anywhere else. I'm sure another school will take me. They can't hold having a drink over my head forever, especially since I'm sure this kind of thing happens all the time. I'm just happy they decided not to press charges, and it's not on my legal record. As for my academic record, it was embarrassing as hell to have to explain that I got kicked out for drinking on campus. But I'll do whatever I have to do.

I've already filled out twenty applications for other colleges. I filled out nearly forty for jobs.

I'll keep applying myself until someone gives me a break. I'm sure my professors are disappointed, but at least they were kind enough to offer their recommendations.

My heart twists in my chest. I hate disappointing people. Especially those I look up to. In my mind, I see Dr. Griffins shake her head slightly, mouth parted in shock as I told her I had to leave.

Disappointed.

Well, you and me both, I guess.

I keep walking down the sidewalk and I start to get a real uneasy feeling creeping over me. It's so fucking quiet. There's no one around. It's just dead. I'm pretty used to walking everywhere, even late at night, but not on this side of town. I don't even know what time it is.

I should be home this late at night. I shouldn't be here. It's obvious this isn't the safest part of town. But I just couldn't go back to the apartment and have nothing to tell Cheryl.

I'm the one who looks out for her. But right now I've got nothing for either of us.

I couldn't tell Cheryl that I didn't get the job, and that I have no plan for us.

She's freaking out about money. She's kind of a wild child, and she's never had a worry in her life. I love her free spirit and all, but that needs to take a back seat when your parents cut you off. She isn't like me though. She's never worked a day in her life. Between all my savings and the scholarships, I was able to pay for college on my own. Not Cheryl Fletcher. I don't think her perfectly manicured hands have ever performed any sort of manual labor. Which is fine if you don't have to, and it's not like she's a spoiled brat who throws it in your face.

But her parents were pissed about the expulsion and completely cut her off. And it's not like she isn't trying-- she's filled out more job applications than I have. Partly because she doesn't plan on going back to school. She was undeclared anyway since she doesn't know what she wants to do with her life.

But the best plan we have to make rent this month is to start selling our shit. And by our shit, I mean hers. A purse or two from her collection would be enough to do it. I'm not going to ask though. My everyday purse is a clutch I bought on clearance from Target a few semesters ago. Hardly glamorous, and hardly expensive. Nope, not like Cheryl's newest purse, a Michael Kors hobo with buttery soft leather. Still, I'm not going to ask and put her in that position.

It's the only option I can think of though.

I see a few guys walking two blocks up from me. They're on the opposite side of the street and heading in my direction. I don't like it. They're talking and laughing, and having a good time. They don't seem threatening. But still, a young girl walking alone and three men... I just don't like it.

There's an alleyway on my left that lets out a few blocks down from the main road where our apartment is. As I stand in the opening, I can see it opens up on both walls of the alley halfway through and that there are some cars farther down on the other side. It's empty.

I don't even hesitate to take the left turn and walk toward more people. Toward safety. I'm pretty sure it's an even faster route home--I think, anyway.

It's dark, and things look different when it's dark.

I pick up my pace with my eyes straight ahead on the light at the opening to the other street.

I'm about halfway through, right near the openings on both sides of the alley when I hear shouting.

My heart jumps in my chest, and my breathing stalls. I instinctively take a step back and nearly fall on my ass with fear.

It's *angry* shouting. More than two men arguing in what I think is Russian. Or maybe German. I don't know. All I know is that I don't understand anything they're saying, and I shouldn't be here. I look behind me for a moment, but I don't know where those three men are. Fuck. Fuck.

I don't know what to do. The yelling gets louder and

closer. My heart hammers faster in my chest. I feel lost and trapped as my throat closes with fear.

I could just run as fast as I can through the opening. It's large enough that a car could get through. But they sound so close. If they saw me, they'd definitely be able to catch me before I made it out the other side.

I take a deep breath and chance a look, just a small glance to see what's happening.

My breathing slows, and the only thing I can hear is my blood rushing in my ears. My heart *thumps*, *thumps*, *thumps* way too loud. They're going to hear me; they're going to see me.

I feel a small sense of relief as I see a row of trashcans blocking the path. I can see past them though. Maybe twenty feet from me, there's a group of men gathered in the parking lot of a warehouse.

I don't know what's going on, but it's not good. So far, no one's spotted me since I'm peeking around the corner with just part of my head showing. I could still get down on the ground, try crawling in the dirt and gravel, and hope I get through unnoticed.

Instead I watch, paralyzed with disbelief at what I'm seeing.

A man's standing apart from the others. It's not the fact that he's in a custom-tailored suit when they rest of them are all in wrinkled khakis or worn-out jeans. He's one of the tallest men, with broad shoulders that stretches the rich fabric tight across his gorgeous frame. But that's not it either. His very presence is a dominating force. It's the air around him.

He's a dangerous man. The other men may be mean,

or even pure evil. But this man is ruthless, calculated, and something tells me he can get away with it. He's a man who isn't denied, and for good reasons. The shadows on his face only make his high and sharp cheekbones even more severe. A light dusting of rough stubble lines his hard jaw.

He's handsome in the most sinful ways, but he'd break you without thinking twice. Maybe even intentionally.

He straightens his crisp white shirt from under his dark navy suit with a gun still firmly in his hand, his finger on the trigger. His barely contained anger is evident even at this distance. He's listening to the man screaming, the one being dragged over on his knees to the center where the other men are circling.

Another man, Ricky, is yelling back. At least I think that's his name, since that's what it sounds like they're calling him. Ricky is obviously in charge of the group of men who are mostly dressed in dark denim jeans, and Henleys or hoodies.

All but *him*.

All of them are under Ricky's control, except the man with the absolute power.

Their guns are pointed at the one man who's unarmed and on his knees. Two men are pushing down on his shoulders, forcing him to maintain that position.

"Fuck you! Fuck all of you!" the man on his knees yells out and spits on the ground.

"So it's true!" yells one of the men holding him down.

"Fucking pig! Fucking liar!" the men are yelling, practically chanting. I realize with a start that the man being forced to kneel must be an undercover cop. I fumble in my clutch for my phone. I need to get help.

"What did you tell them?" asks Ricky. *Bang!* I almost scream and have to cover my mouth with my hands as the sound of a bullet cries out and echoes through the alley. My phone drops to the ground, and the screen cracks from the impact.

My heart stills as Ricky yells out and grabs the cop's shoulder.

Somehow I don't think they heard me, or saw me. Their focus is on the cop who's still on his knees clutching his leg and wincing in pain.

"The next one will be in your skull." Ricky walks closer to the man and puts the gun up to his temple, twisting the barrel of the gun to taunt him. "What did you tell them?"

The kneeling man attempts to laugh although he's in obvious pain. "Just do it. You'll never get anything from me." He sneers as blood soaks through his jeans. It's so dark, it almost looks black.

No! No! I need to do something. As I bend down to get my cracked phone, the man in the dark suit moves forward. A hush falls over the men. The only exception is Ricky, who's cussing and making threats that don't seem to affect the undercover cop.

"Is it true?" a deep, rich voice asks so calmly that it doesn't seem real. The loud click of his gun cocking makes me take a step forward. My head shakes. No. No.

It's silent. Everyone's waiting for his answer, even Ricky.

"Fuck you, you fucking criminal."

"What did you call me?" The man's voice raises with a deadly tone. He points his gun at his target's head.

"You really going to make me say it again?" the man on his knees asks, but his voice cracks. The fear of imminent death is finally coming through.

And with that, his death sentence is complete. One shot, *bang*, and he falls to the ground. The man in the suit moves his arm again and aims at the ground this time. I can't see, but I hear the shots ring out, again and again. *Bang, bang, bang!*

I shake my head with disbelief, tears leaking from the corners of my eyes. They killed him, and I saw the whole thing. My blood runs cold, and the sickness I'm feeling threatens to come up my throat.

And then I do scream. I shriek louder than I ever have before.

A pair of hard, unforgiving arms wrap around my waist and chest before a hand covers my mouth. I struggle against what feels like an unmoving brick frame holding me tight, my back to his hard chest. Caught. I've been caught. I fight for my life; my nails dig into his skin, piercing and scratching. But it does nothing. He's so much taller than I am, so he easily picks my body up off the ground and wraps his hand around my throat, suffocating me. I struggle as much as I can. But it's hopeless, I'm already losing consciousness. The last thing I see, before my world goes black, is the man in the suit looking down the alley. His intense gaze is focused solely on me.

ALSO BY W. WINTERS

Read Willow's sexiest and most talked about romances in the Merciless World

This Love Hurts Trilogy
This Love Hurts
But I Need You
And I Love You the Most

An epic tale of both betrayal and all-consuming love...
Marcus, the villain.
Cody Walsh, the FBI agent who knows too much.
And Delilah, the lawyer caught in between.

What I Would do for You (This Love Hurts Trilogy Collection)

A Kiss to Tell (a standalone novel)
They lived on the same street and went to the same

school, although he was a year ahead. Even so close, he was untouchable.

Sebastian was bad news and Chloe was the sad girl who didn't belong.

Then one night changed everything.

Possessive (a standalone novel)

It was never love with **Daniel Cross** and she never thought it would be. It was only lust from a distance. Unrequited love maybe.

He's a man Addison could never have, for so many reasons.

Merciless Saga

Merciless

Heartless

Breathless

Endless

Ruthless, crime family leader **Carter Cross** should've known Aria would ruin him the moment he saw her. Given to Carter to start a war; he was too eager to accept. But what he didn't know was what Aria would do to him. He didn't know that she would change everything.

All He'll Ever Be (Merciless Series Collection of all 4 novels)

Irresistible Attraction Trilogy

A Single Glance

A Single Kiss

A Single Touch

Bethany is looking for answers and to find them she
needs one of the brothers of an infamous crime family,
Jase Cross.
Even a sizzling love affair won't stop her from getting
what she needs.
But Bethany soon comes to realise Jase will be her
downfall, and she's determined to be his just the same.

Irresistible Attraction (A Single Glance Trilogy
Collection)

Hard to Love Series
Hard to Love
Desperate to Touch
Tempted to Kiss
Easy to Fall

Eight years ago she ran from him.
Laura should have known he'd come for her. Men like
Seth King always get what they want.
Laura knows what Seth wants from her, and she knows it
comes with a steep price.
However it's a risk both of them will take.

Not My Heart to Break (Hard to Love Series Collection)

Shame On You Series
Tease Me Once
I'll Kiss You Twice

Then You're Mine
Tease me once... I'll kiss you twice.
Declan Cross' story from the Merciless World.

Spin off of the Merciless World
Love the Way Series
Kiss Me
Hold Me
Love Me

With everything I've been through, and the unfortunate
way we met, the last thing I thought I'd be focused on is
the fact that I love the way you kiss me.

Secrets & Submission (Love The Way Series collection)

Extended epilogues to the Merciless World Novels
A Kiss To Keep (more of Sebastian and Chloe)
Seductive (more of Daniel and Addison)
Effortless (more of Carter and Aria)
Never to End (more of Seth and Laura)

Sexy, thrilling with a touch of dark Standalone Novels

Broken (Standalone)
Kade is ruthless and cold hearted in the criminal world.
They gave Olivia to him. To break. To do as he'd like.
All because she was in the wrong place at the wrong time.
But there are secrets that change everything. And once he
has her, he's never letting her go.

Forget Me Not (Standalone novel)

She loved a boy a long time ago. He helped her escape and she left him behind. Regret followed her every day after.

Jay, the boy she used to know, came back, a man. With a grip strong enough to keep her close and a look in his eyes that warned her to never dare leave him again.

It's dark and twisted.

But that doesn't make it any less of what it is.

A love story. Our love story.

It's Our Secret (Standalone novel)

It was only a little lie. That's how stories like these get started.

But with every lie Allison tells, **Dean** sees through it. She didn't know what would happen. But with all the secrets and lies, she never thought she'd fall for him.

You Are Mine Series of Duets

You Are My Reason (You Are Mine Duet book 1)

You Are My Hope (You Are Mine Duet book 2)

Mason and Jules emotionally gripping romantic suspense duet.

One look and Jules was tempted; one taste, addicted. No one is perfect, but that's how it felt to be in Mason's arms.

But will the sins of his past tear them apart?

You Know I Love You

You Know I Need You

Kat says goodbye to the one man she ever loved even though **Evan** begs her to trust him.
With secrets she couldn't have possibly imagined, Kat is torn between what's right and what was right for them.

Tell Me You Want Me
A sexy office romance with a brooding hero, **Adrian Bradford**, who you can't help but fall head over heels for... in and out of the boardroom.

Small Town Romance
Tequila Rose World

Tequila Rose Book 1
Autumn Night Whiskey Book 2
He tasted like tequila and the fake name I gave him was Rose.
Four years ago, I decided to get over one man, by getting under another. A single night and nothing more.
Now, with a three-year-old in tow, the man I still dream about is staring at me from across the street in the town I grew up in. I don't miss the flash of recognition, or the heat in his gaze.
The chemistry is still there, even after all these years.
I just hope the secrets and regrets don't destroy our second chance before it's even begun.

A Little Bit Dirty

Kiss Me In This Small Town

Contemporary Romance Standalones

Knocking Boots (A Novel)

They were never meant to be together.
Charlie is a bartender with noncommittal tendencies.
Grace is looking for the opposite. Commitment.
Marriage. A baby.

Promise Me (A Novel)

She gave him her heart. Back when she thought they'd
always be together.
Now **Hunter** is home and he wants Violet back.

Tell Me To Stay (A Novella)

He devoured her, and she did the same to him.
Until it all fell apart and Sophie ran as far away from
Madox as she could.
After all, the two of them were never meant to be
together?

Second Chance (A Novella)

No one knows what happened the night that forced them
apart. No one can ever know.
But the moment **Nathan** locks his light blue eyes on
Harlow again, she is ruined.
She never stood a chance.

Burned Promises (A Novella)

Derek made her a promise. And then he broke it. That's
what happens with your first love.

But Emma didn't expect for Derek to fall back into her
life and for her to fall back into his bed.

Valetti Crime Family Series:
A HOT mafia series to sink your teeth into.

Dirty Dom
Becca came to pay off a debt, but **Dominic Valetti** wanted
more.
So he did what he's always done, and took what he
wanted.

His Hostage
Elle finds herself in the wrong place at the wrong time.
The mafia doesn't let witnesses simply walk away.
Regret has a name, and it's **Vincent Valetti**.

Rough Touch
Ava is looking for revenge at any cost so long as she can
remember the girl she used to be.
But she doesn't expect **Kane** to show up and show her
kindness that will break her.

Cuffed Kiss
Tommy Valetti is a thug, a mistake, and everything
Tonya needs; the answers to numb the pain of her
past.

Bad Boy
Anthony is the hitman for the Valetti familia, and damn
good at what he does. They want men to talk, he makes

them talk. They want men gone, bang - it's done. It's as
simple as that.
Until Catherine.

Those Boys Are Trouble (Valetti Crime Family Collection)

To Be Claimed Saga
A hot tempting series of fated love, lust-filled secrets and
the beginnings of an epic war.

Wounded Kiss
Gentle Scars
Primal Lust
Broken Fate

Collections of shorts and novellas

Don't Let Go
A collection of stories including:
Infatuation
Desires in the Night and Keeping Secrets
Bad Boy Next Door

Kisses and Wishes
A collection of holiday stories including:
One Holiday Wish
Collared for Christmas
Stolen Mistletoe Kisses

All I Want is a Kiss (A Holiday short)
Olivia thought fleeting weekends would be enough and it

always was, until the distance threatened to tear her and **Nicholas** apart for good.

Highest Bidder Series:

Bought

Sold

Owned

Given

From USA Today best selling authors, Willow Winters and Lauren Landish, comes a sexy and forbidden series of standalone romances.

Highest Bidder Collection (All four Highest Bidder Novels)

Bad Boy Standalones, cowritten with Lauren Landish:

Inked

Tempted

Mr. CEO

Three novels featuring sexy powerful heroes.

Three romances that are just as swoon-worthy as they are tempting.

Simply Irresistible (A Bad Boy Collection)

Forsaken, (A Dark Romance cowritten with B. B. Hamel)

Grace is stolen and gifted to him; Geo a dominating, brutal and a cold hearted killer.

However, with each gentle touch and act of kindness that

lures her closer to him, Grace is finding it impossible to remember why she should fight him.

View Willow's entire collection and full reading order at willowwinterswrites.com/reading-order

Happy reading and best wishes,
Willow xx

ABOUT WILLOW WINTERS

Thank you so much for reading my romances. I'm just a stay at home mom and avid reader turned author and I couldn't be happier.
I hope you love my books as much as I do!

More by W Winters
www.willowwinterswrites.com/books/

Sign up for my Newsletter to get all my romance releases, sales, sneak peeks and a **FREE** Romance, **Burned Promises**

If you prefer *text alerts* so you don't miss any of my new releases, text
US residents: Text WILLOW to 797979
UK residents: Text WWINTERS to 82228

Contact W Winters
Bookbub | Twitter | Goodreads | Tiktok
Instagram | Facebook Page | Website

Check out Willow Winters Wildflowers on Facebook.